Enjoy!

Tales of the Monkey King

by

Teresa Chin Jones

Illustrated by Miki Harris

Pacific View Press
Berkeley, California

Cover design: Jos Sances

 Address inquiries to Pacific View Press, PO Box 2897, Berkeley, Ca 94702. Visit *www.pacificviewpress.com.*

Library of Congress Catalog Card Number: 2007052954
ISBN: 978-1-881896-30-2

Printed in the United States

Library of Congress Cataloging-in-Publication Data
Jones, Teresa Chin, 1944-
Tales of the monkey king / by Teresa Chin Jones ; illustrated by Miki Harris.
p. cm.
ISBN 978-1-881896-30-2
1. Folklore--China--Juvenile literature. 2. Monkeys--Folklore--Juvenile literature. I. Harris, Miki, ill. II. Title.
GR335.J66 2008
398.20951--dc22

2007052954

Contents

Introduction

I hope that you enjoy reading these tales to the children in your life as much as I enjoyed writing them. These are based on the Monkey King Tales as I remember them from my childhood. This immensely long and complex set of tales has been part of Chinese culture from at least the tenth century. There are as many versions as there are storytellers. The text that I've written is merely a plot framework for you to embellish.

For those of you who would prefer an authentic Chinese scholar's version, I recommend:

The Adventures of Monkey, by Wu Ch'eng-en, translated from the Chinese by Arthur Waley. Wu Ch'eng-en probably lived between 1505 and 1580 A.D. and wrote the version he knew from his time. Waley's translation is condensed but includes the best-known episodes. For those who are comfortable reading French, the French translation by Louis Avenol, titled *Si Yeou Ki* ("Voyage to the West") covers all the episodes, including a few that are more an excuse for pedestrian poetry or Buddhist dogma than anything else. So my apologies go to any academic purists, and my hope is that each generation will add more life to the tale as they tell it again. This may be one of the longest fairy tale cycles in the world. Even better, it is one where little girls don't have to wait for their Prince Charmings and where little boys can slay monsters without having to marry the princess and end up with the burdens of ruling a kingdom.

The tales are set in the China of myth—the Middle Kingdom. It is a universe where Buddhas have achieved enlightenment; where a Celestial Emperor and his mandarins (officials) manage the affairs of men; where saints must fight monsters and souls seek rebirth. Animals are not just animals. Animals have souls, and some even achieve supernatural powers—joining a pantheon of were-beasts (known as *jing* in Chinese) such as fox-jing, or were-fox, and snake-jing, or were-snake. Like humans, some jing are good and some are evil. Magic permeates everything. All living beings are bound in eternal cycle of life and death, birth and rebirth, but good triumphs over evil.

CHAPTER 1

Beginnings

A stone monkey is born, finds a monkey tribe, becomes king, and seeks to learn the secret of immortality from a Great Sage.

The story of Monkey begins with a large stone. Back when the earth was created, this stone fell from the heavens, landing in the Middle Kingdom in the land of Ngao Lai. For eons, the stone rested quietly on the peak of the Mountain of Flowers and Fruits. For eons, the sunlight engendered life in the stone until, one day, the stone cracked like an egg. Out bounded a monkey. Born full-grown, he was an average-looking monkey, curious and active, like all monkeys, but not, on first sight, anything really special. He gave himself the name "Stone Monkey" and, feeling hungry and a little lonely, he set out to explore. A few days later, just as he was beginning to feel very lonely (monkeys are social creatures) he came upon a large troop of monkeys. He immediately joined them, and was content. The monkeys, who called themselves the Monkey Tribe of the Mountain of Flowers and Fruits, had no real home, but spent their days roaming their mountain, playing and searching for food. Each day flowed into the next—day by day, season by season. But one day in midsummer, the troop came to an enormous waterfall barring their way between two mountains.

"What's behind the water? Can there be treasure? Could there be monsters?

Whoever is brave enough to explore deserves to be our King!" they chattered.

Meek monkeys hid in the trees. Brave ones climbed a cliff. From its edge they could see two rainbows glistening in the spray. Stone Monkey took a deep breath. Without hesitation he flung himself through the waterfall. His monkey friends screamed in terror.

To their surprise, and probably his, he didn't drown. He landed on a stone ledge on the far side of the crashing water. From the ledge, an iron bridge led to an enormous marble pavilion set in a cavern. Marble tables held bowls of fruit. Marble chairs stood invitingly. Carved on the pavilion's marble entrance were the words "Mountain of Flowers and Fruits, Land of Happiness, Cavern of Waters." This was a monkey paradise.

Whooping with joy, Stone Monkey leapt back through the "water curtain" and invited the troop to their new home—a home clearly designed just for their happiness. The excited troop immediately elected Stone Monkey their king. As any newly chosen Middle Kingdom emperor would have done, he took a new name, "Mei Hou Wang," meaning Perfect Monkey King. He lost no time in appointing monkey dukes, monkey ministers, and monkey officials. Soon his court would have been recognized by anyone from the Middle Kingdom's Imperial Court. It was certainly just as full of busy officials scurrying back and forth.

And just like the Middle Kingdom's Imperial Court, a major duty of the monkey court was to hold important celebrations. One day during a celebration involving play, carousing, singing and dancing, and the drinking of much fermented peach juice, an old monkey minister suddenly collapsed.

"Alas, our Great Minister for East Mountain Peaches has reached the end of his cycle. His spirit now will be judged. May he be reborn to the rank he earned because of his virtuous life," the monkey chamberlain told Monkey King.

Now, kings are so busy that they don't notice as much as they should. For years, Monkey King had seen new monkeys born and noticed old monkeys disappear, but this was the first time he realized that these old monkeys had DIED. Horrors! Could it happen to him? From that day, he no longer enjoyed eating, drinking, or playing. It seemed that being king did not exempt him from the cycle of life and death. His mood was so dark that the entire troop became depressed. Their fur no longer shone. Instead of leaping from branch to branch, they crept along the forest floors. Finally, a group of monkey ministers went to consult a sage monkey who had lived longer than all of them and was famed for his wisdom.

The sage came to address Monkey King:

"Your weeping and wailing have distressed your subjects. Your duty as king is to hearten them, not to worry them. Indeed, all beings and even all objects have a beginning and an end. All living beings are subject to the endless cycle of birth and rebirth. Only those of extraordinary virtues who have lived thousands of pure lives can climb higher on the ladder of life until they are freed from the endless chain of birth and death. Those who do, become saints, immortals, and even Buddhas."

"O, Monkey-Sage, your words are true but I am a stone monkey, born of a stone. Why should I be subject to the cycle of birth and rebirth? Is there any way to become immortal?" asked Monkey King.

"O, Great King, only a few great sages and magicians have achieved immortality, even though many can live ten thousand years. You are not like the others in our monkey-tribe, so you may succeed. But you must find a Great Sage and become his disciple. Perfection in anything—even freedom from death—can come only from learning," the sage monkey advised.

So, Monkey King decided to leave his kingdom and search for a Great Sage. He appointed his most trusted monkey duke as regent, to care for the kingdom. The monkeys built him a boat so he could follow the river away from the kingdom. They stole human clothes for him to wear and filled his boat with dried fruits. Monkey King was about as tall as a ten-year-old boy, and walked upright. With clothes covering his light brown fur, and a cap on his head, and with his tail tucked discretely down a pants leg, he looked more or less like a very hairy boy. If you saw him, you would think him very odd-looking, but you wouldn't have to run screaming to your mother.

For nine years Monkey King wandered from mountain to mountain, from village to village, from river to river, looking for a Great Sage who could teach him the Way to Immortality. There were magicians, there were charlatans, there were sages, there were priests with magical powers, but no Great Sages. Reaching a dark, dense forest at the very border of the Middle Kingdom he lost heart and decided to return home. But, on the last day, as he prepared to turn back, he heard someone chanting a mantra. Through the brush, he could see a woodsman casually chopping down trees with his bare hands. Amazed, Monkey King leapt out and knelt before the man.

"O, Great Immortal Sage, accept me as your disciple. Your powers are beyond compare," he prayed.

The woodsman laughed so hard that he fell over.

"Strange monkey being, I am no sage. I am, as you see, a woodsman. I have a family and an aged parent to support. Years ago, I was injured. We would all have starved if the Great Sage who lives in the Cavern of the Moon on this mountain had not taken pity on me. Not only did he cure me, he taught me a mantra to keep me strong and to allow my hands to fell trees. Go to him if you seek learning."

He took Monkey to the gates of the Cavern of the Moon where the Great Sage and his students lived. Monkey King knelt at the gates.

"Great Sage," he said, " to come to you, I crossed rivers and mountains and seas. I never slept in one place twice for nine years. I am no ordinary monkey but was born of stone. I am King of the Monkey-Tribe on the Mountain of Flowers and Fruits. I beg you to accept me as a disciple."

Now, the Great Sage was all-knowing. Of course, Monkey King was destined to be his pupil. Though he put on a stern face, he allowed Monkey King to enter. Monkey King was given a stern lecture on the very strict regimen at the school and told to accept the humblest and dirtiest tasks. As Monkey King had no human name, the Great Sage named him. He was given the clan name "Hou" ("monkey" in Chinese), and the last name of "Souen" and first name of "Wu Kung" ("he who penetrates the void with thought").

Chapter 2

Monkey Develops His Powers

Monkey King makes friends,
masters secret lore, and is forced to return home.

Monkey King, now Souen Wu Kung, began his student life assigned to the humblest tasks. He swept, gardened, cleaned, and obeyed the Great Sage and all of the students, even the youngest and lowest. Since he was always lively and cheerful and took jokes played on him with good humor, he soon made many friends. He was a clever student, too. What he heard, he understood immediately. To him, the most complicated mantras and arguments were transparent as glass.

Seven years passed. He had mastered everything that the Great Sage had taught He could write so well that he could probably have passed the Middle Kingdom Imperial Examinations and achieved the rank of Imperial Governor. But he was no closer to reaching immortality. He was bored and very, very restless. Monkeys are quick and twitchy by nature. Even miraculous stone monkeys find it almost impossible to sit still. One warm summer day, he was so bored that he began to twitch, scratch, rub his nose, and bounce up and down on his bench.

Seeing this, Great Sage said to him, "You can't sit still. You should tell us what it is you wish to master. Do you wish to learn the future, or to know the paths of good and evil?"

"Either one is fine if it will give me immortality," answered Monkey King.

"Oh, no, no. I can't offer that. But I can teach you letters, medicine, divination, kung fu, and all the arts," explained the Great Sage.

"Anything is fine, so long as it will make me immortal," said Monkey King.

They went back and forth for some time. The Great Sage offered ever more complex knowledge but Monkey King was fixed on immortality as his sole goal. Finally, the Great Sage's face turned purple with anger. Scowling, he hit Monkey King three times on the head with his staff, and turned his back on him. The other students were terrified, but Monkey King didn't seem very bothered, although he did stop twitching.

That night, after everyone else was asleep, he crept into the Great Sage's bedroom. The Great Sage snored happily away. Monkey waited as patiently as he could, but finally began humming, clearing his throat, and clicking his teeth. The Great Sage awoke with a start.

"Wu-Kung, you idiotic, twitchy ball of monkey-hair! What are you doing here? Up to no good, I'm sure," growled the Great Sage.

Not the least abashed, Monkey King answered politely:

"I am a humble student and would never presume to trouble you, except for your invitation. When you tapped me three times, I knew the third hour was the time. Since you tapped me on the head, I knew it was to teach me. When you turned your back, I understood that you wanted me to come in secret. So, here I am. But I will wait, until morning if necessary."

The Great Sage was pleased. He had never had a human student who was so astute. Though Monkey King had monkey traits and monkey failings, he did not have many human failings. He could be vain, rash, angry, and impatient, but he was not greedy. He didn't hunger for power. He didn't envy others. He didn't desire beautiful females, or fine foods, or fancy palaces. Monkey King loved knowledge. He wanted admiration and loved to show off, but had no interest in forcing others to kneel to him. Knowing Monkey King's supernatural origin, the sage could sense the hand of destiny. He knew that his teaching would be important. But, since he was not himself a Buddha, he could not know just how.

For three years, Monkey King came each night in secret. He learned how to transform himself into seventy-two different kinds of beings. He was taught how to become as large as a mountain or smaller than a gnat. He learned how to sky-vault, to go up to ten thousand li (Chinese miles) in a single leap. His strength became immense, and his flesh harder than steel. In fact, he became so skilled it really pained him that he couldn't show off just a little. One evening as all the students were relaxing on the verandah of the school, one of his friends remarked how beautiful the pine tree in front of the school was.

"Too bad there aren't twin trees there. It looks so lonely," he mused.

Monkey couldn't resist a chance to show off. So he changed himself into the tree's twin. Everyone applauded and cheered, making so much noise that the Great Sage came out. The Great Sage was not amused.

"Vanity, vanity, vanity . . . Idiot fur-head, what about your promise? Now that you have demonstrated your secret learning, the others will be envious and angry if I do not teach them. I cannot blame you for acting according to your nature—which, despite this lapse, has much that is decent—but you must leave."

Monkey King was shattered, and begged and begged for another chance, but it was too late. He had to go. The Great Sage's parting warning rang in his ears.

"If ever you tell any being that I was your teacher—if you even whisper one word—I will personally skin you, rip out your lungs and your innards and reduce you to mush. My last word of advice is to remember that power is not wisdom. Follow Heaven's path and you will find enlightenment."

Monkey's return to the Mountain of Flowers and Fruits took just seconds. Armed with his new knowledge, he had only to leap through the clouds. (This maneuver is called a "sky-vault" or "to climb a cloud ladder"). It was good to see the Mountain of Flowers and Fruits again. But as his subjects gathered at the foot of the mountain, they began to weep and wail.

"O Great King, why did you abandon us so long? Without you to protect us, a monster called the Phantom Prince, has taken over the Cavern of Waters. He chased us all out. He raids all over the mountain and takes your subjects prisoner. Many monkeys have been killed and eaten. We are helpless. He comes and goes like the wind."

Monkey King's heart swelled with sadness and anger. He leapt into the clouds and, using his far-seeing eye, he immediately saw a monster sign—a black, noxious, vapor. Monster vapor was invisible to humans.

Monkey King leaves to find the Great Sage with secret of immortality.

Monkey, however, could see the auras of all living things, both natural and supernatural, from the black clouds of were-monsters to the rainbow halos of saints.

Not the least bit afraid, and maybe, in fact, even a bit happy to have a chance to test his powers, Monkey King strode up to the mouth of the Cavern of Waters and thundered in a voice loud enough to shake the tables and chairs inside the pavilion,

"Come out and fight, you worthless evil vermin. I, King of the Monkeys, Souen Wu Kung, challenge you to a duel."

He didn't wait long before the Phantom Prince and his monster generals came out, resplendent in gold and bronze armor. Phantom Prince was at least twenty feet tall. Even his shortest general was eighteen feet tall. In fact, they were all so tall they looked right over Monkey King's head and missed him entirely.

"Show yourself, false Monkey King! I am the only royalty here," shouted the Phantom Prince.

"Here, you idiot! Have you no eyes?" screamed Monkey King, so angry at being ignored that he was bouncing up and down like a yo-yo.

Phantom could see him now—a skinny monkey frothing with rage and bouncing like a ball. In fact, Monkey King looked so funny that Phantom Prince almost split his armor laughing. Not the least bit impressed, he tossed away his battle-ax and decided to beat Monkey King to a pulp with his staff. After all, what would be the honor in chopping up such an insignificant foe? He'd just look silly using an ax.

Size isn't everything. Monkey King was small, but he was very, very fast. And his fists and feet were like steel. Before Phantom Prince could even touch him Monkey King had beaten him black and blue. No longer amused, Phantom Prince took up his ax. He would turn that monkey into minced monkey meat. But before he could even swing his ax, Monkey King made himself twenty feet tall. Worse yet, he transformed 300 of his hairs into copies of himself. The Phantom Prince and his fellow monsters were surrounded. In seconds, Monkey King had cut Phantom Prince in half, killed his generals, and put the monster army to flight. Charging into the Cavern of Waters, he freed all the monkey prisoners. After a grand funeral for the monkeys who had been killed and eaten, and a big cave cleanup, the monkey tribe happily settled back into their Cavern of Waters.

Chapter 3

Defeating the Underworld

Monkey King arms his kingdom and finds the right war staff for himself. He is called to the underworld and wreaks havoc. The Celestial Emperor decides to act.

Now reestablished in his kingdom, Monkey King lost no time in improving his rule. From his study of human history, he had learned that a weak kingdom invites attack. Even a rat isn't afraid of attacking a toothless lion. To make his kingdom secure, he drafted young monkeys, taught them to use weapons, promoted the best to be officers, and appointed generals. Next, he created a furious sandstorm so that all the humans in the valleys next to the Mountain of Flowers and Fruits were forced to hide in their cellars. He transformed ten thousand hairs into little monkeys and sent them to the human armories to steal all their weapons. Now the monkeys had helmets, armor, swords, spears, bows, arrows, and battle-axes. The monkey soldiers practiced and drilled until they became a formidable—if somewhat odd looking—army. The Monkey Kingdom of the Mountain of Flowers and Fruits became so strong that the seventy-two monsters that lived in the vicinity came to kneel before Monkey King. What a sight, to see a parade of were-foxes, were-boars, were-bears, were-turtles, and other were-beasts make obeisance. Were-beasts were greatly feared. In the Middle Kingdom, just as there existed great human sages and magicians, sorcerers and practitioners of black magic, so there existed animals that had achieved great powers. These were called "jing" in Chinese, but we will just call them were-beasts, or monsters. Though capable of taking many shapes, they always reverted to their true shape when defeated or killed.

Not all jing were evil, even though we are calling them monsters. Some chose to live apart from all other creatures in order to follow the path of perfection and so achieve eventual sainthood. Some even lived among people and used their magic to heal and help. Others, however, lived to do evil. They increased their power by eating their victims and taking the victims' life force. Each monster, whether evil or good, had a magical talisman that was the core of their power. And all had very great powers. "To have seventy-two jing come to my court," thought Monkey smugly, "shows just how high and powerful I have become."

Monkey King was now supreme throughout his land. A Monkey Kingdom parade was a fine sight, with well-dressed officials and fully armed soldiers. But Monkey King himself dressed simply in a student's cotton robe. And he carried no weapon.

"This is getting silly. I don't care a fig for clothes and my bare hands are stronger than weapons, but I've had to fight much harder than necessary against monsters because I don't look impressive. It's no good trying to transform myself into a thirty-foot-tall monkey. I just scare my own subjects to death. I might even trample a few by accident," Monkey King declared to his council.

"Sire, no human-made weapon is strong enough for you. What good is a sword if you bend it or a spear if it breaks when you throw it? Perhaps our neighbor, Dragon King of the Eastern Sea, whose armory is beyond compare, may have something useable," advised his minister of war.

A monkey king could act faster than any human king, because monkeys had not yet learned the need for debate, consultation and reports in triplicate. In one sky-vault, Monkey King reached the palace of the Dragon King of the Eastern Sea. Muttering a water-spell, Monkey King, walked underwater to the Dragon Palace. Although challenged and attacked by both a fierce pike general and a brave crab colonel, he brushed them aside, tied them up with seaweed, and announced himself to the Dragon King and his court.

"Great Dragon King, I, Monkey King of the Mountain of Flowers and Fruits, have come to pay my respects. I would have come sooner to fulfill the courtesies, but I was busy subduing the neighboring monsters and training my army."

Normally, such a presumptuous hairy thing would have been beaten and thrown out, but no one dared. They had already seen Monkey King swat aside a fearsome pike general and a ferocious crab colonel. The dragon king decided to make the best of it. Though fearsome-looking, he was really a peaceable sort who preferred to enjoy his wine, his dragon-wives and his amusements.

"Welcome royal brother. We are always ready to offer a feast to a new visitor," he said.

"If I had the time, I would gladly dine with you. Since I eat only fruits, nuts, and rice and I don't like seaweed, it would just put your kitchen to too much trouble. I came to beg a favor. Your armory is famed throughout the Middle Kingdom. Even Celestial soldiers are not as finely equipped as your warriors. Can I ask for the loan of a good weapon?" asked Monkey King.

This was a bit direct for the Dragon King, who was used to hearing fawning speech from his courtiers. But he decided that, in view of Monkey's battle skills, a bit of tolerance was in order. The "loan" of a weapon seemed a very small price to pay to rid himself of this hairy pest. After all, he didn't have to fear an invasion of monkeys in his kingdom, and he was flattered that his armory was so well known. So he and his court took Monkey King to look at weapons. Monkey King was thrilled and didn't know what to try first. He was so strong that swords crumpled in his grasp, spears broke, bows were destroyed, arrows bent and axes fell apart. Even a one-ton trident was tossed aside as if it were made of paper. After testing, but destroying, dozens of the Dragon King's best weapons, he began to look quite irritable, frowning and chewing his lip. This really terrified the court. Things didn't look very good. Just then, the very learned Dragon Queen spoke up.

"Great Lords and Magnificent Monkey King, when I was a princess in the Western Ocean, I learned that at the border of the Eastern and Western seas is a large iron column, left there by Buddha when the oceans were formed. Once used to sound the depths of the oceans, it has lain there for a million years. Perhaps, it would withstand your testing."

The whole court traveled to the column. It was certainly large—over 100 tons in weight and 1,000 yards long. Monkey was already an expert stick fighter, and his favorite weapon was the staff. He transformed himself into giant-monkey size, then hefted the iron staff. It felt perfect—balanced, flexible, and heavy. However, he didn't want to go around at his current size just to be able to use it.

"It's perfect, but much too large and thick. To use it, I'd have be so big that I wouldn't be able to set foot on shore without destroying whole cities," he sighed.

At his words, the staff began to shrink until it was just the right size for a normal Monkey King. Great! He could now read the inscription at its base: "Always sized to fit your needs." Delighted, Monkey King made it fat, made it thin, made it longer, made it smaller and finally, since he preferred to have his hands free, he reduced it to the size of a pin, which he put inside his ear.

"Great Dragon King Brother—your generosity is surely that of a brother—I would like to make another small request. As a king yourself, you know that royalty has a duty to impress not only subjects but other kings. This creates harmony and keeps bullies from temptation. Though I would happily wear only a scholar's cotton robes, I have a duty to show a worthy imperial face for my kingdom. Can you lend me some royal robes, maybe some royal armor?"

Feeling very nervous about Monkey King's powers, Dragon King was eager to comply and even more eager to get Monkey King out of his ocean. But his spare robes and armor were tailored for a dragon shape. They weren't going to fit very well. Dragon Queen again gave the right advice.

"Honored husband, your brothers have magical armor and robes that will take any shape. Those clothes are gaudy and gilded enough to please this Monkey King pest. Your brothers should turn over their clothes and armor to Monkey King. We will file a complaint with the Celestial Court and we'll get everything back. Why should we fight Monkey King when it's the duty of the Celestial Emperor and the Celestial Army to do it?"

So, messengers were sent to the dragon kings of the Northern, Southern, and Western seas. Each rushed to the palace with helmet, armor, and embroidered robes. These were presented to Monkey King. They were magnificent—of gold, decorated with precious stones. The chain mail shone like the sun. The robes were embroidered with designs showing Heaven and Earth. Monkey King was so excited that he barely remembered to say thank you before sky-vaulting, dressed in his new finery, back to his own throne room. He spent days showing off his new war staff—felling trees, powdering boulders with a blow. His finery was so magnificent (though occasionally a bit scratchy) that he was confident he could dazzle any ambassadors. Visiting were-beast kings acted even more humble when they saw proof of Monkey King's great powers.

Work, play, endless monkey chatter, and great feasts . . . time flew by. One day, when Monkey King was happily napping after drinking too much peach wine, he dreamed that two men approached. Each wore a headband embroidered with the words "Harpooner of the Dead." One held a silver cord. The other carried a paper with the name "Souen Wukung" written in fine calligraphy. The men tied the silver cord around his neck and with one quick jerk, pulled his soul out of his body. These men, messengers of Yen Wang (Emperor of the Shadowlands, Ruler of the Dead) rushed him to the great citadel of the Underworld. Here the souls of the dead were judged. After judgment the dead would suffer in Purgatory according to the merit or punishment decreed by their actions in past lives until their rebirth. Rich men could be reborn as poor slaves. Criminals could be reborn as beasts to suffer pain and slaughter. The virtuous were reborn to happier lives. The evil would be reborn as vermin.

Kings aren't much used to being manhandled. Such disrespect. Such surprise. Monkey King was furious. His was no ordinary soul, and he still had his iron war staff (which being supernatural, was not left behind with his body). With a great roar, he broke the silver cord. Using his staff as a club, he rampaged through the entire citadel, knocking down walls, pulverizing furniture, and breaking many arms and legs. He laid low hundreds of underworld demons ("kwei" in Chinese) with what he considered light little taps, but which broke their bones anyway.

"Save us! Save us! A fierce monkey-shaped demon is destroying the city," they cried.

Even the Lords of the Shadowlands were too weak to stop him. Finally, to save the rest of the city from annihilation, they knelt and begged him to stop.

"O Great Lord, please, please, stop destroying our citadel. We were only doing our part in the great chain of birth and rebirth. With no death, there would be no rebirth. Souls would no longer ascend the chain of being."

"How dare you kidnap me from my kingdom! I, a stone monkey, cannot possibly be subject to your control," thundered Monkey King, making his voice so loud that even buildings shook.

"If there was an error, we will correct it. Don't beat us further! It wasn't our fault," the lords wailed.

"Cowards! The lord is always responsible for the actions of his officials. You will take me to the Great Book of Life and Death and show me what is written there," answered Monkey.

So they came to Hall of Records. In the Book of Life and Death, he found the following inscription: "Souen Wu-kung, stone monkey, engendered by sunlight and moonlight, will die in his sleep at age 342."

"Nonsense, who gave a clerk the right to decide," said Monkey, as he grabbed a writing brush and blacked out his name. For good measure, he also blacked out the names of all his subjects (which is why there are some very long-lived monkeys in the Middle Kingdom). Satisfied, Monkey King leapt out of the Shadowlands and flew back to his body. He awoke to find his entire court, sure that he had died, mourning him and making preparations for a grand funeral. Although he didn't mind listening to all the eulogies, he decided he would rather be alive. Little did he know his troubles were just about to begin.

Although the workings of the universe and the cycle of birth and rebirth have to do with Buddha, the concerns of Earth, with its many kingdoms and lords, clearly requires more hands-on administration. For this, there was a Celestial Emperor, who ruled from the heavens, and a Celestial Court filled with various saints and Celestial mandarins and generals. Every day, the Celestial Emperor held court. Any of his subjects could come to him for justice and help. So, as Monkey King left the Underworld, the Dragon Kings of the East, West, North, and South oceans arrived at court to file a formal complaint against a monstrous Monkey King who had extorted one iron staff, one royal helmet, one suit of royal armor, and one set of Heaven-Earth embroidered royal robes. They had just finished when Yen Wang, Emperor of the Shadowlands, appeared to file his own complaint against one Souen Wu-kung, also known as Monkey King, for destruction of property, destruction of official records, and assault and battery against demon-subjects. These were serious charges, any one of which could bring severe punishment from the Celestial Emperor. The emperor's assistants were very alarmed.

Though Thousand-Mile-Seeing-Eye Saint, responsible for arrests, was ready to bring Souen Wu-kung in chains for judgment, Pole-Star Saint spoke on Monkey King's behalf:

"Great Celestial Emperor, we should not act as they do on Earth. We should not punish without attempting to correct. All beings can achieve perfection by leading a life of virtue and reform. This Monkey has avoided evil for over three hundred years and achieved miraculous learning and power. His origin is supernatural. He has the power of transformation, and he has vanquished evil monsters and protected his subjects. Rather than arresting him, be merciful. Bring him to our Celestial Kingdom and give him a minor job. Here, he can improve his manners. And if he should behave badly, we can easily correct him."

The Celestial Emperor was moved. Indeed, Monkey King had potential. He just needed to learn more manners and control. So Pole Star Saint was sent to call on Monkey King. Monkey King was overjoyed to think he was being honored for his life of virtue and he accepted his appointment to a position in the Celestial Kingdom. Besides, after 342 years of peace and monkey-chatter, life had become a bit boring. Leaving his ministers, dukes, and generals in charge, Souen Wu-kung followed Pole Star Saint to the Celestial Palace.

Chapter 4

"Great Saint Equal of Heaven"

Minister of Horses Souen learns his true rank and names himself "Great Saint Equal of Heaven."

Souen was formally appointed Minister of Horses. He was put in charge of a magnificent marble stable, more beautiful than the Tang Emperor's palace, with one thousand horses, each in its own marble stall. At his approach, the horses all lowered their heads. Bowing down, his staff hailed him as their new master. Though Souen was a king, monkeys aren't much on etiquette. He had never before been treated with such respect and courtliness. This was Heaven indeed.

Monkey King, both superior to and more energetic than all other monkeys, got right to work. First, he put the stables in order. Working his heavenly staff around the clock (heavenly beings don't need sleep), he soon had one thousand sleek, strong horses who had never been so well tended. Now he had time and energy to spare. He spent it gadding about all over Heaven. He was no snob. He was as happy to chat with celestial sweepers, maids and stable hands as with Great Saints and Mystics. Though friendly, Souen had no idea of heavenly court etiquette. After all, as king of his own kingdom, others knelt to him. Soon he was popular with all the less important heavenly beings. But he shocked all the celestial ministers by his manners, his refusal to prostrate himself, and his lack of awe and respect. Though irritated, as heavenly beings they were too polite to correct him. So, Monkey King continued in his informal ways. He did, however, begin to get an idea of the heavenly hierarchy.

One day he asked some other officials, "To what rank does my title correspond?"

"This appointment, Sire, is the highest in the royal stable. It is outside the Royal Hierarchy," was the tactful answer.

"Above it?" asked Monkey King.

"Not really. It's what you do before entering the hierarchy at its lowest level. You will be praised if the horses do well and will be chastised if they do not. With luck, you can hope for promotion in a few years," they explained.

Hearing this, Souen ground his teeth with anger. The veins on his head throbbed.

"What contempt they show me! What a sap I was! I, who am King of the Mountain of Flowers and Fruits, am now reduced to the rank of a lowly stable hand. Well, I'm not staying!" shouted Souen. He took his iron staff, stormed out of the Celestial Gates and returned home.

His monkey troops were stunned to see him. Fifteen years had passed for them, although only fifteen days had passed for him. He told them of his humiliation at being turned into a stable hand. Better to be a king in his cavern.

As Monkey King was as powerful as ever, his court began to gain more attention from all the regional vassal monsters. One, Great One-Horn, who was Monkey King's General of the Forward Guard, flattered Monkey King's vanity by suggesting that his title should have been "Great Saint Equal of Heaven" instead of chief stable hand. Delighted with the idea, Souen immediately ordered new banners with this title.

By now, the news was out in the Celestial Empire. The Minister of Horses had deserted his post. Angered, the Celestial Emperor Chang Ti ordered his troops to arrest Monkey King for dereliction of duty. General Li, Guardian of the Gate, General Kia, General of the Forward Guard, and Generals Tou and Tcha of the Right and Left Flanks all descended to the Mountain of Flowers and Fruits and demanded Souen's instant submission.

They hardly expected any trouble from a monkey, even a Monkey King, so they were stunned when Souen Wu Kung came out in his dragon armor and thundered:

"I could have killed all of you with just one blow of my iron staff, but I'm merciful. Lackeys, running dogs, go back to your master and tell him he doesn't know how to make use of talented sages. Read my banner. From now on I am to be known as 'Great Saint Equal of Heaven!' "

Furious, General Kia tried to cut Monkey King in two, but one blow of Monkey King's staff shattered his sword. Another blow, and he collapsed on the ground. If he had not been a Celestial general, he would have been hamburger. The other generals could barely manage to retrieve him and escape. They retreated back to the Celestial Court. This humiliation was too much. Prince Na Tao decided to see to Monkey King's punishment personally. The prince, unfortunately, looked like an eight-year-old boy, although he had fearsome powers. When he issued a formal challenge, Monkey King laughed so hard he almost fell off his throne.

The powerful prince began combat by transforming himself into a giant three-headed, six-armed warrior, armed with a sword, ax, war staff, mace, spear, and lasso. Seeing this, Monkey did the same except that his six hands held six iron war staffs. The prince then transformed himself into a thousand-armed warrior. Not only did Monkey King do the same, but he transformed one of his hairs into another thousand-armed warrior. The two then attacked the prince from both sides. This was too much. The prince fled. Monkey King gleefully added the title "Great Conqueror of Heaven" to his banners.

Since Monkey King had done no real evil, Pole Star Saint still had hopes of Monkey's reform. He urged the Celestial Emperor:

"This monkey being has no regard for proper ways and is used to violence, but he is not evil. Show him mercy and he will reform. What are titles? Let him keep his title of "Great Saint Equal of Heaven." The title carries no real power. Just invite him now and then to your feasts. Living in your Celestial Kingdom and granted your mercy, he will learn the proper way and he will surely reform."

Unlike earthly emperors, the Celestial Emperor was not so small-minded as to bear grudges or care about a minor disrespect. So it was decreed. Pole Star Saint came again to the Mountain of Flowers and Fruits and said:

"I should have explained better. I can understand your disappointment. It was never meant as an insult to your abilities. I have persuaded Chang Ti to forgive you for deserting your post. He invites you to return to Heaven. He is even kind enough to let you keep the title 'Great Saint Equal of Heaven.' As this is a new title, you will, of course, be outside the hierarchy."

Returned to Heaven, Souen was given a palace with two pavilions and the job of Controller of the Celestial Peach Orchard. He also had several Immortals under his command. At last he was content. But in his kindness, Pole Star had not explained the "reform" part of the proposal. Souen was under the impression that he, a powerful Monkey King, had received no more than what he deserved.

CHAPTER 5

Havoc in Heaven

The Great Saint steals peaches and cinnabar.
Celestial soldiers go to war against him.

Monkey King was now master of a magnificent palace. "Palace of the Great Saint Equal to Heaven," announced the gold carving on his front gates. With two Immortals assigned to do all the work, he was free to spend his time visiting other palaces, gossiping with Celestial princes, generals, saints, Constellation Immortals, Star Immortals, and anyone who would pass the time of day. The sight of the friendly, sociable Monkey King gadding about became familiar to everyone. In fact, he did so much visiting and chatting that soon no one else could get any work done. A quick whisper as passed to the Celestial Court. In no time, the Celestial Emperor gave him more duties and promoted him to be the "Chief Guardian of the Celestial Peach Orchard," responsible for the welfare of each tree. As monkeys love fruit, this was like assigning the fox to guard the henhouse.

The Celestial Orchard had 1,200 trees that bore fruit every 3,000 years. With just one bite of a 3,000-year peach, one achieved immortality, suppleness, and strength. Another 1,200 trees bore fruit every 6,000 years. One bite of a 6,000-year peach added the power of flight to immortality. In the rear of the orchard, another 1,200 trees bore fruit every 9,000 years. One bite of a 9000-year peach gave not only immortality but the same length of life as for the sun, moon and stars. Nine thousand years had just passed. The fruit of all 3,600 trees was ripe. To celebrate this astounding occasion, the Celestial Empress prepared to host a Celestial Peach-Tasting Banquet.

Now, no one had warned Monkey King that the peaches were to be picked for a Celestial Peach Banquet. Nor had anyone invited him. He, however, was a fruit-loving monkey and had never smelled such wonderful peaches. He forgot he was only the guardian, not the owner of the garden.

"One taste couldn't do any harm," he thought. He tasted one. It was so wonderful that he quickly ate another, and another, and another, until he had eaten every one of the ripe peaches. He was terribly thirsty, so he drank several large jars of celestial wine. Now he was very drunk, and very sleepy. So, he reduced his size to two inches, settled onto a tree branch, and snored happily.

Meanwhile, the Celestial Empress had ordered her handmaidens to pick the ripe peaches for the banquet. But, when they entered the orchard, the handmaidens shrieked in horror. There was nothing on the trees but a few green peaches. Their screaming woke up Souen. Taking the role of the stern Peach Orchard Garden Guardian he thundered:

"Stop all that noise! What are you thieves doing here in my Peach Orchard?"

"Oh, Great Saint, we are not thieves. The Celestial Empress herself sent us here to pick peaches for the Once-in-9000-Years Peach Banquet," they sobbed.

"No one told me about a banquet. Just who is invited?" demanded Monkey King.

"Oh, everyone who is important, sir," they answered. " All the Ministers, Sub-Ministers, Assistant Sub-Ministers, Deputy Assistant Sub-Ministers, Saints, Immortals of the First, Second, and Third Grade, and Heads of Departments."

"What about me—Great Saint Equal of Heaven—who has a unique rank outside of the hierarchy and should certainly outrank a nest of bureaucrats?" Monkey shouted.

"We saw no invitation for you. Perhaps there has been some oversight. Maybe the messenger angels were slow."

Monkey King was truly furious by now. His eyes burned red. His chest swelled with anger. He could barely breathe.

"How can I not be invited! No excuses, now. This is the Celestial Realm. Unlike earthly realms, bureaucratic errors do not happen." He fixed the handmaidens with a spell, the fix-in-place spell, that rooted them to the spot. He would take his revenge for this insult.

Changing himself into a fly, he flew to the banquet hall in the Palace of Celestial Clarity. He stared angrily at the elaborately set tables, the innumerable jars of wine, the thousand-and-one dishes of fine foods and of course, all the servants bustling about with name cards, golden chopsticks, and the finest porcelain dinnerware. There was no name card for him, even at the humblest sub-ministerial table. Monkey King grew even angrier. He decided to have his own banquet, so he cast another fix-in-place spell on all the servants. Seating himself on the Celestial Emperor's chair at the head table, he helped himself to the best of the wine and food.

Soon he was thoroughly drunk, although not stupidly drunk. Transforming himself into the likeness of a Celestial herald, he intercepted all the guests who were on their way and announced to them that the banquet location had been changed to another palace. This bought him some time.

Then, the hangover began. A terrible skull-splitting headache. A mouth drier than a desert. A belly on fire, and a ringing in his ears. What pain! Only Lao Tze, Great Immortal Celestial Physician, could help. Somehow, he managed to crawl to Lao Tze's workshop. Lao Tze was away teaching his disciples new elixir recipes. No one stopped Souen from entering the inner laboratory. He saw endless rows of gourds containing Lao's treasured Celestial Cinnabar Pills. The special pills had taken Doctor Lao ten thousand years to make. They tasted wonderful, so Monkey King ate every one. These sobered him completely.

But now he knew he was really in trouble. He had no desire to be lectured on his bad manners or to be punished. So using a spell of invisibility, he took a few jars of Lao's best wine, and returned to the Mountain of Flowers and Fruits.

It took twelve hours for the spell on the Celestial Handmaidens to fade. Stunned and shocked, they ran to the empress and reported Great Saint Equal of Heaven's criminal action. They arrived to hear the servants from the banquet hall, also freed from the spell, sobbing about the horrible mess left by Great Saint. Even worse, other servants were reporting to the mortified Celestial Empress that her guests had been waiting for hours and hours in another palace.

No one knew where the Great Saint was.

Gnashing his teeth with fury, the Celestial Emperor, Chang-Ti, immediately sent an army to the Mountain of Flowers and Fruits to bring Great Saint back for trial and possibly execution. Monkey King was not in the least bit concerned. After all, living in the Celestial Realm, he'd seen some less-than-Heavenly behavior. He seized his iron war staff and put the Celestial soldiers to flight. It wasn't hard. None of them wanted to be turned into minced meat just to arrest a food thief. Next, the Four Celestial Kings and Twenty-eight Star Immortals led another Celestial attack. This time Monkey King's generals were captured. Still unconcerned, Monkey merely transformed thousands of his hairs into Monkey Warrior copies of himself that chased all the Celestial troops away from the Mountain of Fruits and Flowers. So ended the first day of combat.

CHAPTER 6

Monkey's Defeat and Imprisonment

Kuan Yin intervenes. Eul Lang defeats Monkey King. The Great Saint escapes the Oven of Eight Trigrams but is finally imprisoned under the Mountain of Five Elements.

The Celestial warriors and Immortals knew that their powers alone were not enough to defeat Monkey King. Only Buddha and the Lesser Buddhas (called "pou sa") had such power. They humbled themselves at the gates of Kwan Yin Pou Sa's palace. The Celestial Forces were in total disarray, they told her, and they begged her to help.

Kwan Yin's chief disciple Eul Lang volunteered. Eul Lang, in the form of a red-haired, green-eyed giant, descended to the Mountain of Flowers and Fruits and challenged Monkey King to single combat. Eul Lang had immense powers. He also had a Magic Truth Mirror that showed the true shape of all beings. No matter what shape Monkey took to shake off Eul Lang, Eul Lang, could use his mirror. Monkey King's army fled. Monkey King decided it might be best to run, and fight another day. But when he transformed himself into a sparrow, Eul Lang became a hawk. When he became a fish, Eul Lang became a fish-eating water snake. When he became a squirrel, Eul Lang became a fox. Finally, Monkey King transformed himself into a temple. The door was his mouth; the windows his eyes; and the flagpole, his tail. As temples have no flagpoles, Eul Lang didn't even need his magic mirror to spot Monkey. He called out,

"So, Souen, you've decided to try a new trick. Let's see how you like it when I break down the door and shatter the windows."

Monkey King decided it was time for him to use the spell of invisibility. But Kwan Yin was watching from the clouds. Using her Vase of Purity, she rendered Monkey King unconscious. Her disciples bound him with Celestial chains that even he could not break. They hauled him back to the Celestial Palace for judgment. Would beheading be next?

Lao Tze was really angry at Monkey. He wanted his magical cinnabar pills back. After all, it had taken ten thousand years to make them. He didn't want Monkey King beheaded before he had a chance to get the pills Monkey had eaten. If he could dissolve Monkey's flesh and bones in his magical Oven of Eight Trigrams, he could retrieve his pills. He had Monkey tossed into the man-high oven. The lid was clamped shut, and twelve guards were posted to keep watch for forty-eight days and nights. That should take care of the powerful Monkey, he thought. Normal flesh and blood dissolved in about a minute.

The guards didn't know that Monkey had special powers to counter extreme heat. He merely recited the "cold dragon" spell and settled down for a comfortable nap. Still, he didn't have it all his way. The smoke irritated his eyes so much they turned red permanently. (That's why paintings of Monkey King always show him with fierce red eyes). On the forty-ninth day, Lao's disciples shook the oven and heard sloshing (which they figured had to be the cinnabar rolling around in Monkey's dissolved remains) and opened the top. They were wrong. It was just forty-eight days of Monkey urine. The minute the top was off, Monkey leaped into the clouds. He was in a foul humor and transformed himself into a Titanic Monkey with six arms, six hands and three iron staffs (each turning like a windmill). He was invincible. So terrible did he look that the Celestial Army broke and ran as he neared the Celestial Palace. Chang Ti came out to meet Monkey King and humbly begged him to come before Buddha's Lotus Throne to settle their dispute. Their war risked destroying heaven and earth.

"At last, I meet the real being in charge and will get my due," thought Monkey King. Not the least humble, he stood in front of Buddha's Lotus Throne and spoke of his miraculous birth, of how he attained the longevity of the sun and moon, and of why it was time for those of inferior powers to yield the Heavenly throne to him.

"After all," he challenged, "what gives Chang Ti the right to rule the Celestial Empire for eternity?"

Buddha listened patiently and extended his hand to Monkey King.

"Vault over my right hand, and I will name you the new Celestial Emperor!"

It looked so easy. Monkey King could go one thousand li with a single sky-vault. This was nothing. The hand, meanwhile, grew to fill the sky.

"So that's the trick!" thought Monkey. "Well, two can play at that game. I never said I'd do it in a single vault. I'll just make sure and do ten thousand vaults. By then, I'll have not only gone over his hand but I will reach the end of the universe."

He vaulted so many times that he left a fiery trail, just like a comet. Finally he stopped. The end of the universe was a vast, blank expanse with five enormous columns reaching as far as even Monkey King's eyes could see.

"Well, I'm certainly at the very end of the universe, but how I can possibly prove it?"

He had an idea, and transformed a hair into a writing brush, and another hair into ink.

He wrote, "I, Souen Wu-Kung, Monkey King and Great Saint Equal of Heaven was here first."

Just to be sure, monkey-fashion, he pissed right at the base of the column to REALLY mark that spot. Then, he vaulted ten thousand times, landing back at the foot of the Lotus Throne where Buddha and the Celestial Court were assembled, and grandly announced:

"Now, make me emperor. I not only vaulted over your hand (vast as it was) but I reached the end of the universe. As proof, I not only wrote on the column but pissed right at its base."

"Distance and size are nothing to one who commands the Void. You never left my hand. Smell here," said Buddha and placed his hand in from of Monkey's nose.

Monkey King knew he was beaten. All his powers were not enough before Buddha who commanded the infinite. But Buddha was not only powerful, he was merciful and prescient. He saw how Monkey's great powers could be turned to good. Instead of annihilating Monkey King, he placed his hand over him. Instantly, his hand became an enormous

Monkey King escapes Lao-Tze's oven of eight trigrams.

mountain (the Mountain of Five Elements), pinning Monkey underneath. Only Monkey's head and hands were free. He was powerless to free himself. A temple on the mountaintop held a sacred text. Buddha ordered the local guardian spirits to feed Souen blocks of iron and to give him molten copper to drink. And he said:

"Power and might are not enough to achieve Celestial power. Virtue and goodness, courage and love are needed. You will have to earn your place as a true 'Great Saint Equal of Heaven.' There will be a monk who travels to India to bring the True Scriptures to China. Are you willing to join him and offer your help? There will be hardship and danger, but if you succeed, you will return to the Celestial Kingdom as a pou sa. Do you agree, or do you want to spend eternity under the mountain?"

Monkey made his choice.

"I have no fear of dangers. If this will free me and allow me to take my true place, so be it, I will wait." And so he waited, for five hundred years.

Chapter 7

Buddha's Request

Buddha asks Kwan Yin to chose a worthy pilgrim to bring the True Scriptures to the Middle Kingdom. Kwan Yin recruits two future disciples for the Holy Monk.

Though the people of the Middle Kingdom knew right from wrong and obeyed the laws of the Tang Emperor, they knew little of the True Way. The few scriptures they had were corrupted and often incomplete. Only the True Scriptures could guide their souls from reincarnation to reincarnation until they achieved enlightenment. A holy man was needed, someone willing to make a perilous pilgrimage to India to bring back the true texts to the Middle Kingdom. Buddha gave Kwan Yin and her chief disciple the task of finding the right man.

They left for the Middle Kingdom carrying with them two precious objects—a silk tunic and a monk's staff—to give to the holy pilgrim chosen for the journey.

En route to China, while resting by the River of Moving Sands, Kwan Yin was approached by the river-monster who lived in it. He was an odd-looking sort, but not particularly ferocious. He introduced himself, showing great humility, aware, evidently that he was in the presence of a pou sa.

"Once I was an inhabitant of the Celestial Palace. I even had a title, Official of Screens. At the last Assembly of Peaches, I was careless and broke a crystal cup. As punishment, I was exiled to Earth. Forgetting my Celestial origins, angry at my fate, and tortured by endless hungers, I became a monster, a were-shark. I have eaten many beings. I feel endless pain and despair. Help me!" he begged.

"Your punishment and pain will end when you mend your ways. A Holy Pilgrim will come to seek the True Scriptures in India. Be his disciple. Serve him well and you will regain the Celestial Realm," said Kwan Yin. She hung a necklace made of the skulls of his victims around his neck and ordered him to wear it until the pilgrim came. He took a new name, "Monk of the River of Moving Sands." We will call him "Sandy."

Kwan Yin continued her travels. Suddenly, her path was barred by a fierce giant were-pig who was armed with an enormous rake. With a wave of her hands, she paralyzed him. Lying there, he moaned:

"Forgive me! Once I was a Marshall of the Celestial Veils. I lived in the River of Heaven. One day I drank too much. I was rude and obnoxious and provoked the Moon Goddess. So I was sentenced to exile and to rebirth as a human. But my luck remained bad. Some celestial clerk made a mistake. There I was, reborn not as a human but as a pig. Fortunately I did retain some features of my heavenly origins. I can still assume a human shape. I have learned some magic. But I was so angry at being imprisoned in a pig body that I became evil, consorted with female were-beasts, drank, caroused, and lived on human flesh."

"Stop now! Do not add to your sins! Abstain from human flesh. You can atone for your evil deeds and return to the Celestial Kingdom. But you must agree to become a monk and serve as the disciple of a Holy Pilgrim who will be going to India," said Kwan Yin. She then gave him a religious name of Chu Wu-Neng, though his nickname remained "Pigsy."

Continuing on, she heard terrible groans from the sky. A white dragon that was dangling from the Celestial Vault cried to her,

"Help me! I was once a Prince, Son of the Dragon King of the Western Sea. But in a temper tantrum, I destroyed a magical pearl and was hung here for punishment."

Kwan Yin felt his pain. She persuaded the Celestial Emperor to release him on condition he serve as the Holy Pilgrims's horse.

Finally, she arrived at Chang An, capital of the Tang Empire. To improve her ability to find the right holy man, she and her disciple took the form of two poor Buddhist monks.

Chapter 8

The Young Monk

The birth and youth of Hwan Tsang, who would be chosen as the Holy Monk for the journey to the West.

Before we meet Hwan Tsang the son, we will meet his father and mother. In the thirteenth year of the Tang Emperor's reign, all men of merit were invited to Chang An for the Imperial Examinations. Those who passed successfully would receive appointments to official government posts. A handsome young man, Chen Kwan Jue, placed first. As he was riding through the streets in triumph, he caught a silk ball thrown at him by the daughter of an Imperial Minister. Her name was Delicacy. Her father had allowed her to choose her husband this way. Soon they were married. And soon Chen Kwan Jue was appointed governor of Kang Chen province.

He traveled to his new post with his wife, who was pregnant, and his widowed mother. On the way, his mother became ill, and they stopped at an inn so she could rest. Chen Kwan Jue went for a walk along the river. Suddenly he saw a large goldfish gasping its life away on the river bank. A good man, he threw it back, and thought no more of it. How was he to know the fish was the son of the River Dragon King?

He had been ordered to arrive at his post as quickly as possible. But his mother was too weak to travel. Leaving her with some money, he promised to send servants to bring her to his province as soon as she was better.

He and his wife were such good people that they were incapable of seeing evil in others. To cross the river, they hired a hired a boatman, not noticing all the signs indicating the fellow was actually a river pirate, Liu Hong. While crossing, he threw Chen Kwan Jue in the river. He then forced the wife to pretend he was the real Kwan Jue. Terrified and grief-stricken, she agreed to save the life of the child she was carrying.

Kwan Jue drowned. His body was found by the River Dragon King, who put a "Pearl of Preservation" in his mouth to keep the body from disintegrating. His soul was invited to stay in the River Palace until body and soul could be reunited.

Meanwhile, Delicacy and her false husband arrived at the new post. Delicacy was miserable and wept daily until her eyes were bloody. One day while in the garden, she heard a voice:

"Don't despair. Your son will be a great Holy One. Kwan Yin will watch over him. The River Dragon King has saved your husband. Heaven will keep you young. You and your husband will be reunited and you will be avenged."

Her tears dried. A few months later, she gave birth to a son. Liu wanted to kill the baby but she begged one day of grace. That night, using her own blood, she wrote out her story, and packed the letter and the baby in a wooden chest. Setting the chest gently into the river, she pushed it into the current. To make sure she would know him again, she had cut off the tip of his little toe.

The box floated all the way to the Kin Shan Temple. The baby was rescued by the temple monks, who raised him in love and devotion. When he was 18, he was given the religious name of Hwan Tsang. Tsang was handsome and brilliant—so much so, that the other monks were jealous and teased him about his unknown origin. Finally, he could stand it no longer and begged the abbot to tell him about his past. The abbot, knowing he was ready, gave him his mother's letter. So he went out into the world to look for his mother.

That very night, Delicacy dreamt that the moon shattered and then became whole again. The next day, her servants admitted a young mendicant monk to her mansion. He resembled her husband. He showed her the letter and his maimed toe. Of course, they were both overjoyed. She begged him to go to the village where his grandmother had been left so long ago, and make sure the old lady, who was no doubt dead by now, was properly buried. Then he was to go to Chang An and present her letter to her father, the Minister—his maternal grandfather.

Miracle of miracles, his grandmother was still alive, though now blind and very poor. As she wept for joy, knowing that she had not been abandoned, her sight was restored. Hwan Tsang continued to Chang An where he told the Minister everything. Armed with his daughter's letter, the Minister led troops to remove the false governor, and had him tried and beheaded.

As soon as the River Dragon King learned of this, he reunited Kwan Jue's body and soul and took him to the bank of the river. Once his family was reunited, Hwan Tsang returned to his temple duties.

Chapter 9

The Emperor's Vow

A dragon disobeys Celestial orders out of pride. He begs the Tang Emperor to stay his execution. The Tang Emperor fails and is taken to the Shadowlands, where he vows to send a mission to bring the True Scriptures to his people.

Now, we will go back a little in time to the city of Chang An. There, a river spirit eavesdropped on three fishermen who were boasting about their catches. One said he knew how to choose the best spots. The second said his nets were finer. The third, who had the greatest catch, said he couldn't take credit for it, because it was his fortuneteller (Yuan Jo Chen) who always told him where to go. This fortuneteller was never wrong. The river spirit, immediately ran to the River Dragon King's palace, crying,

"Calamity, calamity, all the fish will soon be taken. There is a fortuneteller who can guide fishermen to all the fish. He's never wrong."

The Dragon King decided to see for himself. Taking the form of a student, he went to the fortuneteller and asked,

"What day will it rain? If you're right, I'll pay you fifty taels (Chinese ounces) of silver. If you are wrong, I'll wreck your house"

This was a trick question, as the Dragon King controlled the local rainfall and he had already ordered half an inch of rain, to fall in the evening the next day.

Yuan answered calmly, "One quarter of an inch of light rain at noon."

Very pleased with himself, the Dragon King returned home, to find a Celestial imperial edict ordering him to rain one quarter of inch at noon the next day. Hating the thought of losing, he listened to his worst advisors, who suggested that Heaven wouldn't be too bothered by a minor change of time and amount. So he made it rain an inch in the evening. Then he returned to the fortuneteller's home and happily wrecked the house. Yuan, however, just sat there looking at him sadly. He said,

"Death awaits you. You are the White Dragon King of our river and have disobeyed Heaven's orders."

Caught out, the "student" felt his heart sink and his belly fill with lead. Trembling, he begged Yuan to save him.

Thoughtfully, Yuan advised:

"Duke Wei, one of the Tang Emperor's favorite ministers, will receive an order from Heaven to behead you tomorrow night. Beg the emperor to help by keeping the duke from his appointment. Once the execution time has passed, Heaven will give you a reprieve."

That night, the Dragon King came to the Tang Emperor in a dream and begged him to help. Pitying the dragon, the emperor agreed to keep Duke Wei occupied past the appointed time. The next day, the emperor ordered the duke to play Chinese chess with him all night. He could hardly execute the Dragon King if he was busy playing chess. So they played chess, and they played chess, until both the emperor and the duke fell asleep. Suddenly, there was an enormous clap of thunder. They awoke to see the bloody head of a dragon fall from the sky.

"Oh," realized the duke. "Just before I woke up I dreamt I beheaded a dragon at the order of the Celestial Emperor."

The next night, the Dragon King's soul seized the Emperor's soul as he slept and took him to the Shadowlands of Death. In the morning, the empress found the emperor dead. The court Wise Men, however, determined that though the emperor appeared to be dead, his body seemed to be still alive. That meant that his soul had been kidnapped and taken to the nether regions, and might still return to the body. So they began a long vigil around the bed.

Meanwhile, the emperor's soul was making its way to the underworld, summoned by the soul of the Dragon King for failing in his promise. On the way, the emperor met his uncle, who had died long ago. The uncle had risen to the rank of "First Class Clerk in Charge of Tang Empire

Book of Life and Death." He decided to help his earthly nephew. When no one was watching, he took a writing brush and changed the age of the emperor's expected death from 33 to 83. The King of the Shadow Lands wasn't even aware that a sleeping man could execute Heaven's orders. So when the clerk pointed out the error in his death date, the King of Shadowlands agreed to return the emperor's soul. The dragon begged the emperor to help him. He asked that prayers from the True Buddhist Scriptures be said to speed the dragon's reincarnation and return to Heaven. On the way back from the Shadowlands, the emperor saw thousands of souls, waiting in torment for rebirth. His heart filled with compassion for these souls, who would not have been there, if they had learned the True Way. But how could the citizens of the Tang Empire learn the True Way, without the True Scriptures? He knew that he had to send a mission to India, in the far West, to bring the true Buddhist Scriptures to China. Just as he made this vow, he suddenly sneezed. He woke to find his entire family and court weeping at his bedside.

He did not forget his vow. He would be a good emperor and a good man. He would bring the True Scriptures to his people so that they could learn the right way of life and move upward in the chain of being.

The pilgrims begin their journey.

CHAPTER 10

The Journey Begins

The Tang Emperor convokes all the monks in the kingdom. Hwan Tsang is chosen to be the pilgrim. He receives the Precious Tunic from Kwan Yin. Disaster strikes. The Pole Star Saint advises the Holy Pilgrim to find a monkey disciple.

The emperor issued an edict, calling all the kingdom's Holy Men and Women to Chang An. For months, holy ones arrived at the capital, expecting honor, power, and glory. Once they learned that the emperor was expecting them to undertake a dangerous journey that would last at least fifteen years, most ran right back to their temples. Others were too old, too ill, or too weak for such a task. Only Hwan Tsang, who already was known as a brilliant religious leader, was dedicated enough, young enough, and strong enough to go. So he was chosen. To test him, Kwan Yin and her disciple (both in the shape of elderly monks) told him horrible tales. The journey would take years. It would cross unknown mountains, rivers, and valleys. There would be savages, wild beasts, monsters, demons, and ogres. Hwan Tsang said,

"The Scriptures would have no value if merely handed to us from above. Only by making the pilgrimage can we prove worthy of them. Yes, I am human and so my flesh is weak and I am afraid. But my soul is strong, and I will go ahead, despite the dangers and perils. It is a miracle that I am alive. Now it is my duty to repay Heaven."

With that, Kwan Yin and her disciple revealed themselves. They gave him a Precious Tunic to wear when he finished his pilgrimage, reached India, and found the True Scriptures. The Tang Emperor provided passports, gold, a dozen servants and a horse for his journey. And he gave him a special bowl, to use when begging for his meals. From that moment on, he was known as Tang Sung, "Monk from Tang."

Tang Sung set out on the twelfth day of the ninth month of the thirteenth year of the reign of the Tang Emperor. At first, travel was easy. The Tang Empire was at peace and the roads were clear. Temples along the way hosted him and his servants with joy. At the border of the Tang Empire, he came to the Great Mountains. Here, he received the first hint of possible dangers ahead. Despite all sorts of dire warnings from local folks, he and his party continued on.

That night, they were ambushed by over fifty monsters. The attack was led by the Were-Bear, known as the Bear Prince. Most of the servants were killed right away. The rest, along with Tang Sung, were captured and tied up, to be eaten later. Tang Sung, dismayed that his journey was cut so short, resigned himself to death, and fell asleep. Suddenly the Pole Star Saint, in the shape of an old man appeared and cut his bonds.

The "old man" said, to a relieved Tang Sung, "Your only hope is to find a disciple with powers equal to this monster. Go to the Mountain of Five Elements. You will find a strange monkey being, who, it is rumored, is waiting for a Holy Pilgrim to free him."

The old man had not only saved Tang Sung, but he had retrieved his baggage, and his horse, and somehow moved him one hundred li further on his route. When the old man vanished, Tang Sung realized that he had been rescued by a Celestial Being.

Chapter 11

Monkey Joins the Pilgrims

Tang Sung meets Monkey King. Monkey kills six robbers. Monkey King leaves in a snit. Tang Sung is given means to control Monkey. Monkey King is tricked into better behavior.

At the base of the Mountain of Five Elements, he met villagers who directed him to the mountain home of the strange Monkey Being. Tang Sung walked for hours, deeper and deeper into the mountains, until he came to an impassable set of rocks. Just as he was about to give up, he heard a voice coming from what looked like a pile of moss- and lichen-covered rocks.

"Who are you, pale and scrawny human monk? What are you doing here?"

Tang Sung then told his whole story and asked:

"Are you the Monkey Being who will help me reach the West?"

"I'm certainly the one," responded Monkey. "And you certainly took long enough. I've been stuck here for five hundred years. I have had only the local guardian spirits and a few humans for company. I made a promise to Kwan Yin and I'll keep it. Go to the top of this mountain. You will see a small altar with a golden book on it. Lift up the book and I will be freed."

It took Tang Sung all day to climb to the top. There he found the altar, but just as he approached it, the golden book flew up to the heavens.

Tang Sung meets Monkey King.

Monkey yelled, " Get down, off the mountain! I am going to free myself! Rocks will fall."

Tang Sung had hardly reached the village, when he heard and felt an enormous rumble. Suddenly, a strange Monkey Being stood upright before him, saluting and asking to be accepted as his disciple.

"Know that I am the King of the Monkeys on the Mountain of Flowers and Fruits. I also carry the title of Great Sage the Equal of Heaven. Five hundred years ago, I revolted against Heaven and was imprisoned here. I promised Kwan Yin that I would atone for my faults by helping a Holy Pilgrim reach the West. As your disciple, I will use my true name, Souen Wu Kung, given to me by my former teacher. I will call you Master as you have accepted me as your disciple."

The next day, the two travelers set out. Suddenly six well-armed brigands (outlaws) attacked them. Monkey laughed. He didn't bother to even fight them. He just stood calmly, as they hacked away.

"Don't worry. They may think they're robbing us but I know they are going to supply us with clothes and food."

"How can this idiotic looking, hairy, monkey-like boy be so strong?" they moaned. Their arms really hurt from all that chopping and hacking. Finally, Monkey King tired of this and tapped each gently with his staff. He'd never fought humans before and he had no idea how fragile they were. They were all killed. Tang Sung , or Master, as we will call him from now on, was very sad to see these deaths.

"The brigands should have been brought to justice, not just killed. We have no right to take their lives. Now that you are a monk, you should behave like one and be more peaceable"

"Pshaw," Monkey answered, "Was it my fault their skulls were like eggshells? And 'peaceable' won't do much against ogres and monsters."

Monkey had been a king, so he was pretty thin-skinned about reprimands. It was one thing to take orders from his former Master, Great Sage, who knew infinitely more than he did, or to accept orders from Kwan Yin or Buddha. It was humiliating to be lectured by a mere monk. Monkey King was seriously irritated.

"Well, guess I don't have the makings of a monk after all. You'll have to make the trip to the West and retrieve the True Scriptures from India with some other being's help. You can't say I didn't try to help you."

Flouncing off, he vaulted into the sky and disappeared, leaving Tang

Sung in shock. But, he thought, "The pilgrimage must go on, even if disciples desert."

Eventually Tang Sung came out of the mountains. A lady was waiting. She held out an embroidered tunic and an elegant monk's hat, ringed with gold.

"This tunic and hat are destined for your disciple. They are magic. Once your disciple puts it on, the hat can not be taken off until you have finished your pilgrimage. If you say a special mantra, the skull-busting spell, the gold circle will contract and give him the 'mother of all headaches.' He cannot escape it, no matter how far he flies. A second mantra will reverse the first. Even good students need their behavior corrected sometimes. Souen Wu Kung will come back to you."

She then transformed into a rainbow and disappeared. Tang Sung realized that it was Kwan Yin who had come to his aid.

Now, Monkey King had gone to visit the Dragon King of the Eastern Sea so he could complain about all the unfair treatment he suffered. The Dragon King reminded Monkey King:

"Brother Monkey King, my sympathy is with you. Who likes being lectured? Even I have to hide from the Dragon Queen on occasion. But you made a promise to Buddha. Remember, humility isn't considered a virtue because it's easy. Try again. It would a shame to lose a chance to become a Buddha just because a Chinese monk has a nagging tongue."

So Monkey King returned. He found Tang Sung in deep mediation.

Monkey King apologized.

"I am sorry. I was wrong. Now I feel ready to be a disciple again. I shared a few drinks with my old buddy the Dragon King of the Eastern Sea. He shared a few thoughts with me. Very helpful."

He even began preparing the noonday rice. He noticed the beautiful new tunic and hat. It was much too small for Master. Monkey loved bright and glittering things, so he begged Master to let him wear them. Master waited until Monkey had put them on, then explained the special properties of the hat and its golden circlet.

"Well, I don't believe that at all," blustered Monkey, very indignant.

Master began immediately to recite the skull-busting mantra. The golden circle around the hat tightened—tighter and tighter. Monkey moaned, groaned, leaped into the sky, and fled ten thousand miles. He could not escape the headache or get rid of the hat. Finally he returned and begged Master to cancel the spell. By now, he had figured out that Kwan Yin's fine hand had been behind this. There was no way that Master, who was as innocent as any baby and totally free of guile, could have come up with such a spell by himself.

"Kwan Yin must have been a pretty harsh disciplinarian when she was still a human princess. Bet her maids had to hop to when she ordered it," grumbled Monkey.

But what was done was done. Monkey King realized he had to be good or suffer.

Monkey King defeats a dragon and finds a horse for Master.

Chapter 12

Kwan Yin

At the Sad Eagle Waterfall, they meet the White Dragon, who steals their baggage and eats their horse. Spirits help the travelers. Kwan Yin helps them replace their mount.

It was now winter. One day, Master heard the roar of a waterfall. A great river crashed from high cliffs. Ocean-size waves threw themselves across the savage current. As Master and Monkey stood gazing at the spectacle and reading the plaque on the shore that identified it as the "Sad Eagle Waterfall," a ferocious dragon boiled out of the water. Monkey managed to shove Master out of the way, but the dragon snatched the horse and ate him, baggage and all. Monkey King leaped into the clouds, trying to spot the dragon, but it had vanished. Master wept in despair. Monkey grumbled about losing this and losing that and asked himself how he could pursue the dragon if he had to guard Master at the same time. From all around them, they heard small voices:

"Great Saint, stop all this mumbling and complaining. It distresses us. Don't worry. Kwan Yin has already ordered us to help. We're known as the local guardian spirits. We will guard Master while you take care of the dragon."

So Monkey rushed to the shore and shouted,

"Rotten, louse-ridden dragon, Give me back the horse and the baggage, or I'll turn you into dragon soup!"

The dragon, who was napping after his dinner, tried to ignore the dreadful shouting. Monkey King transformed his staff into a huge pole and used it to stir the waters, breaking rocks, and churning up the bottom silt. The dragon realized that this pesky Monkey was too powerful to fight. He changed into a river snake and hid in the grass. Monkey didn't feel like searching aimlessly. He asked the local river guardian spirits about the dragon.

"Once this was a calm lake. But Kwan Yin exiled one of the Celestial Kingdom's dragons here. He had been hung from the heavens for eating a pearl from the Dragon King's palace. She freed him, and he is supposed to wait here for a Holy Pilgrim who is traveling to India. Who was to know he'd eat your horse?"

This was clearly Kwan Yin's fault. Monkey sent one of the guardian spirits to ask her to fix it. When she appeared, Monkey complained,

"Getting me to wear this skull-busting hat was a really dirty trick. And it's your fault that our horse was eaten."

Kwan Yin only laughed. She knew how to best deal with naughty beings, even naughty Monkey Kings. She then called the dragon, who came at once with the baggage. He apologized profusely. He would have never snatched the horse if he had known who Monkey and Master were. Monkey solemnly accepted his apology.

Kwan Yin now transformed the dragon into a beautiful horse.

"This horse can swim the deepest rivers, and climb the highest mountains. He will never tire. He will carry your baggage, and Master."

Taking a more serious tone, Kwan Yin said:

"The perils and dangers to come will make this part of the journey seem like just an easy walk. The powers of evil will become stronger, the farther you travel. Demons haunt the mountains. Were-beasts of immense power wait in the shadows. All will all try to keep you from your goal. I will give you these three special pearls to use at the worst moments. And, by the way, please, be sure to announce yourself from now on!"

Monkey King transformed the pearls into three of his body hairs. When he needed them, they would be there.

Master was overjoyed with the new horse and return of the baggage. The travelers offered thanks to Kwan Yin and the guardian spirits. A river spirit, in the form of an old fisherman, whisked them safely across the churning river. They continued through a forested landscape filled with countless elephants, tigers, panthers, and bears.

Chapter 13

Black Wind Monster

Monks of the Kwan Yin Temple covet Master's Precious Tunic. It is taken by the Black Wind Monster. Monkey King finds the thief. Kwan Yin helps trick Black Wind Monster into swallowing Monkey.

As spring arrived, Tang Sung and Monkey King came to the Temple of Kwan Yin, which was also a monastery. At first the monks were terrified by Monkey's fierce, hairy appearance, to say nothing of his red eyes. But Master was so handsome, kind, and well-spoken that they finally allowed them to enter. While the Temple Elder and Master had all sorts of religious discussions, Monkey had fun playing ball with all the younger monks. Now, Monkey had been feeling a bit humiliated that they had to beg their rice from village to village and temple to temple. He wanted them to know that they weren't just ordinary mendicant monks. He couldn't help boasting about their important mission and about the Precious Tunic that Kwan Yin had personally given Tang Sung at the beginning of his journey.

Monkey forgot the old saying, "Show wealth and robbers know whom to rob." Alas, the Temple Elder and his monks, who knew more about religious study than purity of heart, immediately coveted the Precious Tunic.

"Honored travelers," said the Temple Elder, "We are pleased to offer our hospitality, humble though it is. You may sleep in our guest pavilion. Please join us for a meal, too. But, a favor, please? I would like a closer look at that tunic. Might I take it to my quarters where the lamplight is bright enough to let me see the intricate embroidery?"

Master, by nature kind and generous, could see no harm in this. After all, it was a beautiful garment. The temple elder went off with the tunic. Soon, Master was sound asleep, but Monkey heard the monks whispering:

"Let's cut their throats."

"No. Too much blood. Besides, I don't much like the looks of that strange disciple. He seems pretty strong."

"Better yet, burn them to death. We can tell the Tang Emperor that it was all a tragic accident."

Monkey changed into a bee and saw them preparing piles of firewood and stacking it outside Master's door.

"These evil monks deserve to be pulverized, but my master is so tender-hearted, I'll have to think of a kinder way. I don't need another skull-busting headache," he thought. Leaping into the clouds, Monkey came to the South Gate of Heaven and borrowed a talisman to protect Master from the flames. He, of course needed nothing for himself; he was as immune to the flames as the precious tunic. He slipped the talisman's cord around Master's neck. When the monks lit their fire, Monkey created a Great Wind. It made the flames burn so fiercely that the whole temple burned down.

The flames shot into the sky and were seen as far as Black Wind Mountain, home to the Black Wind Monster. Curious, he took the form of a bat and flew to the temple. There he saw monks running around screaming and vainly trying to put out a fire. He also saw a monk sleeping amidst the flames, protected by a talisman, and an odd-looking monkey dressed as a monk. He was especially intrigued to see a small package surrounded by a brilliant halo. Though the halo's light was invisible to human eyes, it was clear to all creatures with supernatural powers.

"A treasure! Finders keepers!" he chuckled, as he flew off with the package.

The fire burned all night. Tang Sung, protected from the flames, slept through all the commotion, but was shocked when he woke up and heard Monkey's explanation. Monkey reminded Master that he had not killed anyone, only punished the monks.

After all, "If men don't kill tigers, tigers will kill men," he said.

The monks were terrified when they saw Master and Monkey unharmed. They tried to return the tunic, but it was gone.

"None of this would have happened if you had not shown off the tunic," said Master. "Now you will have to retrieve it."

While Monkey would have preferred to argue, he had no desire for another skull-buster headache. Interrogating the local guardian spirits, he learned that the Black Wind Monster was the most likely culprit. So he set off to find him. Black Wind Monster, like most monsters, lived in a cave on a mountain.

Monkey, in the form of a squirrel, hid in the bushes at the cavern's mouth. Three monsters approached—one had a black bear's head. Another was in the form of a Tao doctor. The third appeared as a student dressed in a white tunic. (Monkey could see their black auras, so he knew that they were monsters.) Black Bear Head boasted of his success in stealing a beautiful tunic and invited the others to a feast celebrating his coup. He would call it the Feast of the Ceremonial Garb. Hearing that, Monkey King returned to his own shape. Brandishing his iron staff, he screamed a battle challenge:

"Miserable monsters, contemptible thieves, give me the tunic now or I'll reduce you to blood and brains."

Black Bear immediately disappeared in a swirling storm, and the Tao doctor fled to the clouds, while the White Tunic student stayed to fight. He attacked, was killed, and returned to his real shape, that of a white serpent. With these three at least temporarily out of the way, Monkey King challenged Black Wind Monster. Just as Tang Empire generals did, Monkey thundered out a long listing of his powers and titles. Black Wind countered with a list of all his battles. Plus, he laughed at Monkey, calling him nothing but a jumped-up stable hand. They fought all day and night, but neither could win. The next morning, Monkey decided to use his brains. Changing again into a squirrel when he noticed a messenger-monster who was carrying a letter, he killed the messenger and read the letter. The letter, from Black Wind, invited the Temple Elder to his banquet.

Adopting the Temple Elder's shape, Monkey went to the Black Wind Cavern.

"I'm a little early for the feast," he explained. "I was passing by, and by coincidence met the messenger right outside the cavern. Let's see that tunic!"

Black Wind wondered about this. It seemed too much of a coincidence. Better to hide the tunic, he thought. So he did.

Just as they sat down to dine, a soldier-monster reported the dead messenger. So Black Wind and Monkey, now back in his own shape, dueled again. Again, no one won.

"This could go on forever," thought Monkey. Losing no time, he flew to Kwan Yin's Lotus Throne and asked for her help. He even admitted it was his fault for showing off the tunic.

As Kwan Yin and Monkey returned to the cave, they came across the Tao Doctor-Monster. Monkey wasted no time in killing it. (It reverted to a wolf when dead.) Kwan Yin took the form of the Tao doctor and Monkey took the form of one of the Tao doctor's cinnabar pills. The false Tao doctor then presented Black Wind with a "pill" that would add a thousand years to his life. Delighted, Black Wind swallowed the "pill." Immediately, Monkey began to jump around inside his stomach and to use his intestines as a trapeze. Black Wind rolled on the ground in agony, begging him to stop. At this, Monkey King flew out of Black Wind's mouth and demanded the tunic. Black Wind, defeated, returned the tunic, knelt down before Kwan Yin (who had returned to her true form), and promised to renounce his evil ways. So, Monkey returned in triumph with the tunic

CHAPTER 14

Pigsy

Monkey and Master help a farmer deal with a monstrous son-in-law. Monkey subdues a were-pig. Chu Wu Neng (Pigsy) is converted and becomes a disciple.

In the Village of Pines, in the Country of Wu, they came to the rich farm of Ko Lao. Ko Lao was a devout Buddhist and welcomed them somewhat hastily:

"If only I could give you a proper welcome. Disaster has been my lot. I have a lovely daughter, Bluebell. Three and a half years ago, a fellow came to work on our farm. He was a large, solid man, the most wonderful laborer we had ever seen. In a month, he had doubled our production. When he asked for my daughter's hand in marriage, I was delighted and gave my consent. But things changed after that. Day by day, he became lazier. He also became uglier. Now he resembles as an enormous pig. All he did was eat and drink. He used his great strength to bully everyone. Finally, I scolded him. He leaped into the air, gave a great roar, and almost scared us to death. For three years, he has locked Bluebell up in our home. He does nothing but eat and drink and snore. He is obviously a were-pig. We are totally powerless."

Hearing this, Master wept in sympathy, and Monkey offered to help. That same night, Monkey transformed himself into an ant, came through the keyhole and sneaked into the room where Bluebell was held. There, he resumed his own form and told her his plan. Compared to the monster she had married, Monkey was practically handsome, so she hap-

pily agreed to help. With a magic spell, he reduced her to the size of an ant, so she could crawl out under the door. Once outside, he said a spell and she resumed her normal size. Then, with another spell, he changed himself into the very image of Bluebell and waited for her husband to return.

At midnight, a great wind shook the house, and a very fat, hairy, pig-headed creature came to her room.

"Come on Bluebell, are you going to be mean to me again? I haven't had a nice word from you since I locked you up. After three years, you'd think your heart would soften. Haven't I treated you well? It's hard for me to stay in a handsome human shape for weeks and weeks. Why don't you make the best of it and enjoy me as I am, nice and strong. I am not that ugly. My real name is Chu, my nickname Pigsy. I'm from the Cavern of the Bridge of Clouds on Joy Mountain. I command thirty-six modes of transformation, and I have a deadly rake as my magical weapon. You could do a lot worse," said the Pig-Monster.

Now, usually, when he said this, Bluebell would begin to weep, moan, and whine. He'd get irritated and leave. This time, however, she surprised him by saying:

"Dear Husband, you just don't know how my sisters made fun of me after you became so lazy and after you grew so ugly. Well, I'm tired of listening to them. You're right. After three years of being locked in this room, you don't look that bad. My legs hurt from sitting so much. Can you carry me to the bedroom?" the false Bluebell murmured while fluttering her eyelashes. Delighted, the pig monster put her on his back. "Bluebell," who was really Monkey, made herself heavier and heavier.

"Funny, you don't look fatter and you barely eat, but you really are getting heavier and heavier," said the Pig Monster.

By this time, Bluebell had become so heavy that Pigsy was crawling on all fours. Then he noticed that the delicate white arm that was around his neck had become a long, hairy monkey arm, with a long hairy paw. Tricked! Immediately, he shook off Monkey, but one look at this ferocious red-eyed being sent Pigsy, rake in hand, fleeing.

Now Pigsy really did have great powers. Once he had been an immortal, and Marshal of a celestial river. But one day, while drunk, he put his hands on a Celestial maiden and was exiled by the Celestial Emperor to rebirth on earth. Somehow, a clerk made an error. Instead of rebirth as a human, he was reborn as a pig, but a pig with supernatural powers. He had promised Kwan Yin to reform and join the Holy Pilgrim who would eventually appear, traveling to India. In the meantime, he had decided, he might as well enjoy eating, drinking, and carousing as usual. He had no idea that Monkey was the disciple of Tang Sung. But, from his days in Heaven, he remembered that Monkey King was a real terror.

Monkey had no problem finding Pigsy and immediately challenged him to combat. Though he much preferred to sleep, eat, and drink, Chu was no coward, so he came out. After about an hour, he realized that Monkey was stronger.

"What do you have against me anyway? What are you doing meddling in my family life? Look, I doubled the size of the Farmer Ko's lands. His daughter has always been well fed. I never beat her. So why are you bothering me?" Pigsy asked.

"I wasn't meddling. My name is Great Saint Equal of Heaven, Souen Wu Kung, King of the Monkeys on the Mountain of Flowers and Fruits. Even though I am helping my Holy Master, Tang Sung on his pilgrimage to the West to retrieve the Holy Texts, I can't just stand by and let a no-good, lazy, fat pig-jing like you bully harmless peasants."

When he heard this, Chu bent his knee and surrendered.

"I, too, was saved by Kwan Yin. I, too, have promised to help the Holy Pilgrim. I will join Master now, and I will call you my elder brother."

Monkey took him back to Master, who was overjoyed to have another disciple, especially one sent to him from Kwan Yin. Master gave him a new formal name, Chu Ba Dzieh. He kept his old nickname of Pigsy. Now, they were three.

CHAPTER 15

Yellow Wind Pass

In the Yellow Wind Pass, Master meets ill fortune.
Pigsy shows his talents.

After a month's travel, they came to another range of mountains. Monkey King and Pigsy looked scary, so at their approach, the local villagers trembled with terror, and fled. Finally they found an old man who was too weak to run away. Master was able to reassure him. The old man, then convinced the villagers to welcome them.

"About time we had some decent rice. Master barely eats at all. Monkey seems to never feel hunger. They should understand that I can't possible pay attention to prayers and meditation when my stomach is groaning with the pain of emptiness," complained Pigsy.

Monkey was just as glad to see food, because he was very tired of "younger brother's" whines and moans. In fact, he wondered if it might have been better to leave him in his cavern than to have to listen to him carp. That evening, they feasted. Master spoke to the villagers on the Laws of Buddha. Pigsy ate at least ten bowls of rice and ten platters of vegetable stir-fry, and drank six gallons of tea. Monkey ate little but greatly enjoyed the company of the children.

The next day, the villagers begged them not to continue on.

"The mountains on the road to India are full of horrible monsters. We don't even dare go near them to gather firewood. If you don't want to end up in some monster's stew, you'd better turn back. Surely, you've gone far enough to satisfy the Tang Emperor that you really tried."

But they continued without problems until they were stopped at Yellow Wind Pass by a violent storm.

"This is no normal storm. I can smell a noxious monster spoor in the wind," said Monkey. Just then, an enormous were-tiger barred their route.

"Ah, I see dinner for my master, the Great Yellow Wind King. Come along now, and I won't make it too painful," sneered the tiger.

Pigsy reacted quickly, and flattened the tiger with his rake, but it didn't die. Instead, the tiger leapt into the sky. Unknown to Monkey and Pigsy, the fleeing "tiger" was just a magically animated skin. The real monster, exiting the skin, had already changed into a whirlwind. It quickly scooped up Master and the Horse and deposited them inside the Yellow Wind Cavern.

An empty tiger skin, even magically animated, can't go very fast, so Monkey and Pigsy quickly captured it. As Pigsy poked the skin, it collapsed. Monkey realized they had been tricked. Sky-vaulting back to their camp, Master and the Horse were gone. Monkey leaped into the clouds. He could see the black monster cloud over the Yellow Wind Cavern. He and Pigsy shouted a challenge at the Cavern's mouth. Out came Yellow Wind King's Were-Tiger General, leading a huge mob of monster troops (were-boars, were-buffaloes, were-wolves, and were-stags). Before Monkey could begin combat, Pigsy (legs hurting and furious at being tricked into a long chase) killed the were-tiger and threw its body back into the cavern.

This infuriated Yellow Wind. Obviously, if he wanted Monkey and Pigsy killed, he had to do it himself. Armed with his trident, he challenged Monkey to single combat. After thirty bouts, Monkey transformed his hairs into a thousand monkey soldiers to help him. Yellow Wind countered by blowing away all the copies. Then he blew a poisoned wind at Monkey. It was time to escape. Monkey King could barely see. He was so weak that he had to lean on Pigsy. Finally they found a nearby hut inhabited by a very old man. The Old Man told them that the poisonous wind was called the "Wind of Three Obscurities" and only Immortals, Saints, and Buddhas could withstand it. However, he had a magical "balm of three flowers and nine grains." It cured Monkey instantly. Then both hut and man vanished. Once again, Kwan Yin had sent one of her agents to help them.

Monkey remembered the old Tang Empire saying: "A foolish general attacks without intelligence. The rash deserve defeat." He needed to reconnoiter. Transforming himself into a fly, he entered Yellow Wind Cavern totally unnoticed. He found Master chained to a giant cauldron, weeping, and waiting for death. Buzzing around Master's ear, Monkey whispered,

"Don't be afraid. I promise to deliver you, even if I have to drag Buddha himself over to help."

He knew Master would be kept alive until just before the big banquet that night, so Master was safe for the moment. He could hear the monster-chefs talking about Yellow Wind's power:

"No being, not even an Immortal can withstand his poisonous breath. I heard Yellow Wind say that he was only afraid of the Ling Ki Buddha. Only the Buddha with his Flying Dragon Baton could annul the poisonous wind."

Now Monkey knew what to do. He talked to Pigsy, who happened to remember from his days as a Celestial Marshal, that Ling Ki Buddha lived at the Mountain of Meditation, three thousand li to the south. Monkey was there in an instant and politely begged the Buddha's help. Together, they flew back to the Yellow Wind Cavern. The Buddha hid in the clouds, while Monkey lured Yellow Wind out by calling him a foul smelling, ugly, stupid coward. Having defeated Monkey once, Yellow Wind was full of confidence as he leaped out, armed with his trident. Again, when he couldn't beat Monkey by force, he prepared to exhale his poisonous breath. At that moment, Buddha threw his baton at Yellow Wind. Instantly, Yellow Wind was paralyzed and reverted to his true form, that of a giant yellow rat. Though Monkey was all for cutting him into a thousand pieces, Buddha asked Monkey to spare him.

"This rat must be tried and judged before his punishment is determined. Once, he lived a holy life on Meditation Mountain. One day he drank oil from the lamps on Buddha's altar. Fearing punishment, he escaped to Earth, and his rat nature took over."

Now that Yellow Wind King was gone, Pigsy and Monkey had no trouble at all freeing Master and killing all the local monsters. The people in the villages could once again live without fear.

Thus they continued their journey.

Tang Sung rides the dragon horse. Sandy is the Porter.

CHAPTER 16

Sandy

The conversion of Sha Wu Tsing (Sandy).
Pigsy fights at the River of Moving Sands.

It was now autumn. They came to an immense river, so wide that it looked like an ocean. At the shore, they found a marble table inscribed "River of Moving Sands, eighty li wide, thirty li deep. Even a goose feather will not float in its waters." As they stood there, wondering what to do, a ferocious monster wearing a necklace of nine human skulls and armed with a large trident appeared. Monkey immediately grabbed Master and took him to higher ground, while Pigsy fought the monster. Once Monkey had placed Master on high ground, he came back to help Pigsy. Outnumbered, the Nine-Skull Monster dove into the waters.

Now, while Pigsy was expert in water combat, Monkey was more expert on land. Even Pigsy, though, couldn't handle the monster alone, so they agreed on a strategy. Pigsy dove into the waters and challenged the monster to combat. As they fought, Pigsy pretended to weaken and to flee. The monster lost all caution and chased him to shore, where the waiting Monkey leaped out at him. But the monster dove back into the water.

"You were too impatient. Next time, hold up a while. Let this Nine-Skull Monster get farther onto the shore," said Pigsy.

Again Pigsy leaped into the water and again, they fought. Pigsy again pretended to weaken and to flee. But this time, the monster just dug itself into the river bed and refused to be lured out. So Monkey decided to ask Kwan Yin for advice. Kwan Yin explained that the monster was the former General of Screens, Sha Wu Tsing (nicknamed Sandy).

You will recall that this Sandy had been exiled from the Celestial realm after breaking a crystal glass. In fact, he was supposed to join them in their quest for the True Scriptures.

Kwan Yin reminded Monkey that she had told him to always announce himself.

"Do it right this time," she said. Giving him a gourd, she told him to take the necklace from the monster and wind it around the gourd.

Monkey and Pigsy now politely called out from the shore for the monster. They announced themselves clearly,

"We are the disciples of Tang Sung, the Holy Monk who is traveling to India to retrieve the True Scriptures for the Tang Empire."

The waters parted and the monster came forward, in the form of a sad-faced, middle-aged man, who knelt to them and apologized. He begged to be allowed to join them. Master, seeing this as another example of someone choosing good over evil, was overjoyed. Sandy took off his necklace of skulls and wound it around Kwan Yin's gourd. Immediately, the gourd transformed into a large boat. The boat took them across the river in moments and disappeared when they landed on the other shore.

Now, there were three disciples. Master felt ready for any challenge, as they continued their trek to India.

CHAPTER 17

Temptation of Pigsy

Master keeps to his vows. The Four Saints test the travelers. Pigsy is tempted. Pigsy is caught and promises to do better but harbors a grudge against Monkey for not warning him.

They kept strictly to their travels, living by begging or by gathering wild fruits and nuts. This was fine for Monkey, who, like all monkeys, preferred fruit and nuts. It was even bearable for Sandy, who was a serious, dutiful sort, more likely to lecture others than to need to be lectured. Master was normally so deep in meditation and prayer that he had to be reminded to eat. Only Pigsy really suffered. First, as the chief baggage handler, he worked hard. And he was large. Very large. There was more of him to be hungry. As a pig-monster, he had developed quite a palate for rich meats, spicy sauces, and wine, and so he spent most of each day grumbling:

"Elder Brother, Younger Brother, you both are lean, stringy sorts. Not much is needed to fill your tiny bellies. Have you any idea how hard it is to carry baggage when your empty, hollow, stomach groans and cramps up? Even ten bowls of rice won't fill me now. Look at my pale face. It's clear that I will be a rattling skeleton before we get to India."

They were tired of hearing Pigsy complain. They were ready to gag him, tie him hand and foot, and to carry him along with the baggage. Even Master began to feel a touch of impatience. And even Master was a little hungry. Just then they saw a beautiful country villa up ahead.

"Ah, dinner," they thought, and walked faster.

Monkey, with his keen sight, could see a rainbow aura around the villa. It must be supernatural and holy. He decided to say nothing, not wanting to interfere with whatever the Saints had planned.

Several household servants came to welcome them. A beautiful older woman introduced herself:

"Honored travelers, you are in the country of Tong. I am the humble widow Yang. You are the answers to my prayers. Although we are wealthy, it's lonely here. There are no villages around, and my three beautiful daughters have no chance of finding husbands. Stay with us, marry them, and we will devote our lives to making you happy."

Master put his hands over his ears and refused to listen. Monkey King explained that, as a monkey, he had no interest in human females and his Master, as a holy man, was devoted to the chaste life of a monk. And Sandy explained that he had become a monk and could not take a wife. Pigsy thought the offer was wonderful and was tempted But he was afraid he would "lose face" if he gave in, when his companions were so determined to remain virtuous.

He, too, said, "Thank you, but no."

Naturally, the lady was quite angry at their refusal and had her servants bar the gates, leaving them outside. So, despite the lovely smells of good cooking that came from the villa, they would be dining on their usual meager rice rations.

Once they had made camp for the night, Pigsy suddenly declared there wasn't enough forage for the horse and offered to go find more. Since Pigsy always tried to avoid work, this made Monkey suspicious, but he let Pigsy go and followed him, in the form of a bee. Pigsy wandered innocently until he knew he was out of sight, then ran right to the back of the mansion. He sneaked into the garden, where the women were playing.

"Kind ladies, I only refused your offer because I thought you would find my pig snout and large pig ears unappealing. But I can make myself handsomer. Nothing would please me more than to stay here as the husband of whoever will have me."

The giggling women invited him to tour their home. There were too many rooms to count. The food smelled so good that he could hardly remember to look at the three beautiful daughters. The mother interrupted his happy daze:

"Noble Pigsy, all three of my daughters find you adorable and want to be your wife. As women of good family, all three can't marry you.

Each deserves to be chief wife. (Men, in the Middle Kingdom, could take more than one wife, but only the first one was the official one.) As a mother who loves them equally, I can't favor one over another by choosing for them. Why not use the rite of 'Blind Marriage'? We will blindfold you, and you will chase the women. The first one you capture will be your wife."

Pigsy was beside himself. He couldn't wait. They put a blindfold on him and he began to trot around the garden. He could hear the young women giggling and even smell their perfume. But, how hard they were to catch! He kept running into benches, flowerpots, curbs, and rocks. Finally, he gave up and offered to marry the mother instead. She was more appropriate to his age, in any case. She, however, offered another way to choose. She took out three jeweled embroidered tunics (one red, one blue, and one green) and asked him to select one and put it on. He could marry the daughter who had sewed the one he chose. This way, there would be no hard feelings.

No problem. Pigsy picked the bright red one. The moment he put it on, the jacket changed into a net of cords that bound him tighter than a cocoon. The women and villa disappeared.

Monkey had seen the whole thing. Though he could have freed Pigsy right away, he decided that it might be good for him to spend the night "hogtied." The next morning, Master and Sandy were stunned to find the villa gone, though someone had left a huge bag of rice and dried vegetables for them.

A voice moaned, "I'm sorry. I lied. I forgot my monk's vows because the women were so pretty and I was so hungry. Help free me."

After searching the whole area, they found a large, snorting, pig-shaped bundle. It took Sandy an hour to cut the web and to free Pigsy's head. Pigsy looked so tired and sorry that even Monkey (who had a very strong sense of humor) didn't have the heart to laugh at him more than ten or twenty times. Pigsy, though he said nothing, was quite irritated that Monkey hadn't warned him the whole affair was a Celestial test. He waited for a chance to get even.

Chapter 18

Ginseng

On the Mountain of Longevity in the Hermitage of Five Domains, Monkey picks the ginseng fruits and uproots the ginseng tree. Immortal Tao Doctor Cheng captures all of them. Monkey wreaks havoc in the Hermitage of Five Domains. Monkey King finds a way to revive the ginseng tree. All ends well.

After miles and miles, they came to an indescribably beautiful mountain, named the Mountain of Longevity, where the Hermitage of Five Domains was located. This was the home of the Tao Doctor Immortal Cheng. The gardens possessed a miraculous ginseng tree that was as old as heaven and earth. Its flowers took three thousand years to bloom. It took three thousand more years for fruits to grow and another three thousand for them to ripen. Even smelling these miraculous fruits would triple your lifetime. The whole tree had only thirty of them. To human eyes, each looked like a human baby.

Dr. Cheng had left with most of his disciples to attend a banquet at a neighboring Tao Immortal's home. Only two young disciples (Clear Moon, age 1,200 and Pure Wind, age 1,300) were left behind. As Doctor Cheng was prescient and knew that Tang Sung and his disciples were coming, he left strict orders for them to offer Master two of the fruits, and gave the disciples permission to eat two. When Master came, the disciples offered Master two fruits, but Master recoiled, horrified by the baby-like appearance. So he absolutely refused. The disciples, although they didn't show it, were actually quite happy. Why waste two precious fruits on a short-lived Buddhist monk? They could eat them themselves. While the disciples were congratulating themselves on their good luck,

Pigsy, of the big, big ears, eavesdropped on their discussion. Hmmm-mmm. Why waste the fruits on those two young Taoists, he thought. He told Monkey about the ginseng tree. Monkey and Pigsy soon found the tree and the golden hook used to harvest the fruits.

Monkey shook a fruit loose, but it vanished the minute it touched the ground. So he shook loose another three, but caught them in his tunic. Pigsy ate them so fast that he complained he couldn't taste them. Clear Moon and Pure Wind heard him and ran to the tree to count the fruits. Four were missing. Frantic, they ran to Master to ask him if his disciples had taken the missing fruits.

Monkey and Pigsy realized that they had done wrong, but were too ashamed to admit it. But Master saw their guilty looks. Under questioning, Monkey blamed Pigsy for eavesdropping and putting the idea in his head. Pigsy blamed Monkey for stealing the golden hook and shaking the tree. Then they blamed each other for eating the fruits.

Clear Moon and Pure Water realized that they would be held responsible for not keeping better guard on the ginseng tree.

"Thieves, brigands, ungrateful, rotten, corrupt two-faced monks!" they shouted, faces red with fury.

Monkey promptly lost his temper at the insults. After all, it was only a misunderstanding. How could he know the fruits were precious? Well, he would show them a thing or two. He transformed one of his hairs into his image. Then, changing himself into a sparrow, he flew to the garden, where took up his own shape again and knocked down the tree with his iron staff.

Clear Moon and Pure Water continued to lecture the Monkey-hair for some time before they realized that this Monkey seemed a bit too calm. They ran to the tree and found it uprooted. They were so shocked that they fainted. When they came to, they realized they'd need new tactics. So Clear Moon and Pure Water calmly apologized for "miscounting" the fruits, and said nothing about the uprooted tree. Monkey grew suspicious, and rightly so. The young disciples locked Master, Monkey, and the others in the dining room and accused them of destroying the ginseng tree. Monkey had to put a sleep spell on Clear Moon and Pure Water so that they could escape. Master was horrified, though. How could things get so out-of-hand?

Tao Doctor Immortal Cheng returned the next morning, expecting to spend a pleasant dinner talking theology with the Master. When he saw the tree uprooted and heard about the theft of the fruits, he was so furious that his face turned purple. Flying into the clouds, he spotted Master, Monkey, Pigsy, and Sandy resting quietly under some trees. He leaped down from the clouds, brushed aside Monkey's iron staff as if it were nothing and, using his magic powers, he carried all of them in his sleeves back to his hermitage. Binding them with magical cord, he prepared to punish them.

Monkey begged, "Let me take the punishment for all of them. I was the one who lost my temper and uprooted the tree."

This impressed the Tao Doctor Immortal, but didn't change his mind. He told them it would be thirty lashes for each of them the next morning. Now thirty was nothing for Monkey, whose hide was harder than steel, and it wouldn't be much for Pigsy, who had lots of fat to cushion any blows, or for Sandy, who was just plain tough. But one lash would probably pulverize Master.

That evening, Monkey King reduced his size until he could slip free of his bonds. Then he untied his companions, transformed four willow wands into their image and led them out of the hermitage. At dawn, the Immortal prepared to punish them, but saw through the false-figure-trick instantly. Again, he chased the real figures, and again, he caught them in his sleeves. This time he decided to boil them in oil. Clear Moon and Pure Water, really irritated at Monkey and his companions, were happy to set up a cauldron. While they were busy, Monkey managed to free himself. He noticed a large stone lion statue and, giggling, made it into his exact double. Then he reduced himself to the size of an ant and hid nearby. This would be fun, he thought. Once the oil was bubbling happily, Monkey used his powers to have the Monkey-double volunteer to test it first. Clear Moon and Pure Water tossed what they thought was Monkey into the cauldron. They tossed so hard that the stone lion broke the cauldron and splattered them with hot oil. At this point, Monkey resumed his shape and size, and complained in his most petulant tone that all the commotion was disturbing his nap. Now the Tao Doctor Immortal was so furious that not only was his face purple, but his beard stood on end.

Before the Immortal had a stroke, Monkey decided it was time to be serious.

"Please don't be angry. You know that even a saintly being will keep a trace of its origins, and all monkeys love jokes. I understand your fury. Even, if it kills me, I will find a way to revive the tree. All that I ask is that you release my companions, who are innocent."

Tao Dr. Immortal Cheng agreed, but to make sure Monkey would follow through, he made Master promise to use the skull-busting formula if the problem wasn't solved in three days.

It wasn't easy. Monkey King called on all his old stellar spirit buddies from his time as a Celestial official. He checked all the Great Immortals. He even apologized again to Lao Tze, the most famous Tao doctor of all, whose cinnabar pills he had stolen, and begged his help. Alas, Lao Tze could cure everything but trees. Just when it looked like he should expect the migraine of the millennium, he came to the Celestial home of Kwan Yin. She, his last hope, went personally to even higher regions to retrieve a healing balm. Returning with Monkey, she sprinkled the balm over the uprooted tree. The tree shot into the air and planted itself back in the soil. Thirty-one fruits now hung from its branches. The Tao Doctor Immortal was delighted and apologized for his temper tantrum.

After many days of rest and feasting, during which Pigsy almost ate their entire store of food, and Tao Doctor Immortal Cheng, Pure Water, Clear Moon, and all the other disciples were flat on the ground with exhaustion, they left, with everyone's hearty blessing.

Chapter 19

White Bone Demon

Monkey sadly returns to the Mountain of Flowers and Fruits. Master is captured. Pigsy begs the Monkey King to help. Monkey proves he did not murder three people and kills the White Bone Demon. Master apologizes.

They traveled so far that they left all human habitation behind. No more farms, villages, or even hunters. All was wild and lonely. They had finished all their rice. There were no edible plants to be found on the steep slopes. Master was starving. Pigsy's moaning and groaning at night kept everyone awake. Even when he shut up, his stomach made sad, booming, hollow stomach sounds. Sandy, quiet by nature, became totally silent and depressed. Monkey set out, prepared to go far in his search for human habitation. Before he left, he drew a magic circle of protection for all of them with his staff.

Now, this mountain, the White Tiger Mountain, was the cavern-home of the White Bone Demon, an incredibly powerful monster who had a unique ability. He could create bodies, inhabit them, and, if he wished, leave the bodies behind while his spirit flew away. The remains looked just like genuine corpses of people. With this talent, he had fooled many, many travelers.

Remember that jing, or were-monsters, no matter, how powerful or long-lived, are still subject to the laws of nature. Just like humans, they must eventually enter the Shadowlands to be judged on their past. And just like many humans, the average monster would prefer to achieve immortality the quick way, rather than having to atone for its evil deeds. Because of Tang Sung's holiness and the special favor shown him by Kwan Yin, all were-monsters, including the White Bone Demon, believed that they could achieve immortality by eating Tang Sung's flesh. So, Master was in constant danger. The White Bone Demon was just one of the many immortality-seeking monsters that the pilgrims would meet on their journey to the Holy Scriptures.

The White Bone Demon was talented in divination. He had known that Tang Sung and his companions would be coming. When he saw the travelers approach, he hid in the rocks until Monkey King had gone. Creating the body of a lovely young woman, he approached Master, Pigsy, and Sandy.

"My parents saw you coming from far away and sent me to welcome you," he said. "We are the caretakers of the White Lotus Temple. You can eat with us, and spend the night. I thought you would be hungry and brought you some mantou (steamed Chinese bread rolls)."

Pigsy could smell the buns and was already drooling. But Sandy and Master reminded him:

"Has Monkey brother's advice ever been wrong? We promised not to leave this circle of protection until he returns."

While Pigsy was arguing that such a pretty little girl couldn't possibly harm them, Monkey returned. From a mile up, he could see the black noxious vapor (invisible to humans and less powerful beings) that indicated the presence of a monster. Swooping down, he crushed the girl-shaped creature with a single blow. The White Bone spirit quickly vacated the "flesh" and escaped, leaving behind a dead body. It seemed to Master that Monkey had just committed a murder. Fortunately, as Master stood there, open-mouthed, too shocked to react, Monkey was able to explain. Although he was still upset, Master decided to trust Monkey's judgment rather than his own eyes. But he gave Monkey a long lecture on the need to curb his bloodthirsty instincts. This cheered up Pigsy, who still hadn't forgiven Monkey for laughing at him back when he had "failed" the test of the four saints. Pigsy was so happy that he only complained ten or fifteen times about how hungry he was.

The next night, Monkey again put them in a circle of protection and leapt into the clouds to scout the area. Once again the demon reappeared, this time in the form of an old woman.

"Oh, saintly ones," cried the false old woman, eyes full of tears, "have you seen my daughter? My husband and I sent her out yesterday to look for you and invite you to our home. She still hasn't returned. I beg of you, please help me."

Master became really upset. He would have run to comfort her if Pigsy and Sandy had not held him back. He apologized to the old woman and told her his most powerful disciple mistook her daughter for a monster. When she heard her daughter was dead, the old woman began to tear her garments in despair. Just as Master might have done something foolish, Monkey returned. Remembering his promise to use restraint, he thundered,

"The very air stinks of your evil, foul demon. This time, I'll give you such a beating that it will take a year for you to heal."

The "old woman" screamed and turned to run, but Monkey tapped her with his iron staff. This tap immediately pulverized her. The White Bone Monster's spirit left. Now they had another corpse on their hands. Master was really incensed. He was so soft-hearted that he couldn't even kill mosquitoes that were biting him. How could he stand to see a harmless old woman murdered in front of his own eyes? Even Pigsy criticized Monkey for being "too bloodthirsty." Monkey begged forgiveness and again explained himself.

"I did shout a warning," he reminded them. "How was I to know that the creature could be destroyed by one little tap?"

No one was happy, but they all agreed to continue on together.

The next night, after they made camp, Monkey again drew his magic circle before he leaped into the clouds. They had just settled down when the White Bone Monster came again, this time in the form of a frail old man.

"Kind monks, please help me. My daughter is gone and now my wife has disappeared. I beg you to help me find them," he wept.

Master couldn't restrain himself and came out of the circle. Pigsy and Sandy followed him. Just as the monster was preparing to tie them with an invisible magic cord and kidnap them, Monkey appeared out of the sky. With his supernatural vision, he could see the cord. He had to act right away. There was no time for warnings, no time to explain. With one blow of his staff, he killed the "old man."

Like the previous corpses, this one had a "White Bone Demon" tattoo on it. But again Master didn't believe Monkey. And Pigsy, in a moment of very fuzzy thinking, and always eager to get back at Monkey, declared with a sneer that Monkey himself had probably put the tattoo on the corpse, using his magic. So Master refused to pardon Monkey. Pigsy lectured Monkey about disobedience and violence. Only Sandy urged Master and Pigsy to reconsider. He reminded them that without Monkey, they would have little chance of getting the True Scriptures. No matter how hard Monkey tried to explain, Master refused to listen. And, he began chanting the skull-busting spell. Soon Monkey was too busy rolling around on the ground in pain to say anything. After watching Monkey suffer for an hour, Master formally ejected him from their pilgrimage and ordered him to leave, and never to return. So Monkey, very sadly, left. He asked Sandy, who had tried to help, to be extra watchful.

It was a sad and angry Monkey King who returned to his kingdom, the Mountain of Flowers and Fruits. No monkeys welcomed him. They were all in hiding from hunters. His kingdom was in disarray. Maybe it was for the best that he had come home. After much searching, he was able to collect some of his old court around him. He ordered his generals to pile rocks atop all the mountain passes. Then, when the hunters came, he blew a fierce wind. It toppled the rocks, killed the hunters, and closed the passes. Now, he was able to restore his kingdom. The monkeys of course, wanted to hear the story of his return. They listened, spellbound, as he told how was expelled because of a monster's cunning, Pigsy's lies and Master's too-trusting nature.

Meanwhile, Master, Pigsy, and Sandy continued on. It became Pigsy's duty to be the advance scout and to find food. At first, he loved this, and felt very important. He also had occasional opportunities to sample potential meals. But he soon tired of all the extra work and began to regret his role in pushing Monkey out of their group. One day he was so tired that he fell into a deep sleep under a tree. When he didn't return, Master sent Sandy out to look for him. Master was now alone. Restless and afraid, he walked a little further on the path. Soon he came to a temple, with the words "White Lotus Temple" carved in front.

As Master was marveling at this sight and thinking, "Pigsy and I were right after all. Here's the temple that the girl mentioned," he was seized by the White Bone Monster (in his true shape) and his monster soldiers. They tied him firmly to a pillar and spread the good news to all the monster kings in the region.

Meanwhile, Sandy, hearing loud snoring, had located Pigsy. The two returned to find the Horse and their baggage, but no Master. Following the path, they, too, came to the temple. It didn't look right. Where was Master? Worried, they tried to enter, but there were too many monster guards. They had to retreat.

Master, tied up inside, wept over his fate, while the little monster creatures taunted him:

"Don't cry. You won't taste very good all dried out. Our master, the White Bone Demon, has promised us a bite. Right now, he is trying to decide whether to roast you or stew you."

Pigsy and Sandy weren't sure what to do. They decided to hide near the temple. Pigsy was delighted at how well he had done, even though he had not been able to enter the temple. He kept boasting about his exploits. He boasted so much that he got very thirsty. Looking for something to drink, the two found an old wine cellar full of wine. Pigsy drank five or six gallons and promptly went to sleep. When monster soldiers appeared, Sandy couldn't wake him. Even the shrieking and thumping sounds of the fight that followed didn't wake him. The monsters captured them both and bound them to pillars next to Master. Only the Horse was left behind.

Remember, the Horse was really a dragon. He, too, had magical powers, although ordinarily it wasn't his job to use them. But now, realizing that everyone had been captured, he transformed himself into a mouse and crept into the temple. While the monsters were sleeping, he went to Pigsy's pillar, scampered up Pigsy until he reached his shoulder and whispered:

"It is I, your humble horse, using what little magic I have. I can chew through your ropes. Please, quickly get Monkey Brother. He is the only one powerful enough to fight the White Bone Demon."

Pigsy was not about to argue. Losing no time, he vaulted into the sky and in seconds was in front of Monkey's throne. Monkey was in his full imperial regalia. He looked very fine, indeed. Banners with "Great Saint Equal of Heaven" hung from flagpoles. Hundreds of minister monkeys, court lackey monkeys, soldier monkeys, and such scurried about. Petitioners knelt at the foot of this throne. Remembering that Monkey probably had reason to hold a grudge against him, Pigsy humbled himself and joined the kneeling petitioners.

Monkey had known that Pigsy was coming as soon as Pigsy leapt into the clouds, but he pretended not to recognize him.

"Who are you, you odd looking thing? What's a fat and ugly pig doing wearing monk's clothes? What do you want?"

At this, Pigsy kowtowed even lower. With his snout right on the ground he said,

"Oh, it is so sad how soon brothers are forgotten. It is I, Pigsy, your younger brother monk. I came to ask you to return. Master missed you so much that he's willing to take you back."

Pigsy didn't want to admit that they were in dire straits, or that Monkey had been right.

"Idiot!" Monkey shouted, "I can tell you're lying. Now tell the truth or I'll feed my court monkeys some pork. Old and rancid as your meat may be, it would be a change from fruits and nuts."

Pigsy broke down and told the whole sad story. He also paid up all the apologies that he owed Monkey for every malicious thing he had ever said to Master about him.

So, Monkey returned with Pigsy. He quickly freed Sandy. Then, he transformed himself into the very image of the White Bone Demon's wife. Monkey had a plan.

Speaking as the wife, he said to White Bone Demon, in Master's hearing:

"Dear husband, I am amazed at your daring, but I'm also afraid. Isn't this Tang Sung guarded by a ferocious Monkey King, the Great Saint Equal of Heaven? How did you manage to capture him?"

The White Bone Demon was delighted at a chance to show how clever he had been.

"Give me some credit. Wits are worth more than might. I have a special talisman, a great White Pearl. When I hold it in my mouth, I can create bodies and inhabit them. Let me show you."

First he took the shape of the girl, then the mother, and then the father. He then left the three bodies on the ground and returned to his own shape.

Can you imagine how Master felt when he saw this? Tears rolled down his cheeks as he wept in mortification and regret. He had wronged Monkey, his truest disciple.

The White Bone Demon then gave the Pearl Talisman to the "princess" to examine. As the false princess snatched the pearl, she changed back to Monkey and challenged White Bone Demon to combat. Monkey and the White Bone Demon fought sixty bouts. Pigsy took on, and defeated the White Bone Demon's General of the Left. Sandy defeated the General of the Right. All the little monsters had long since run away. Just when Monkey was about to crush White Bone Demon with the iron staff, he disappeared. Six times, the monster vanished when Monkey was about to crush him. The seventh time, Monkey King waited until White Bone Demon began to weaken. This time, Monkey used his iron staff to crush the talisman. The pearl talisman was the key. It held the life force of the monster. With it crushed, the monster died and an enormous white tiger, his true shape, appeared. Thus, Master was saved and the travelers were reunited. This time, it was Master's turn to admit that he was wrong and to beg forgiveness.

Chapter 20

Five Talismans

On Peace Mountain, a guardian spirit warns of perils. Monkey catches Pigsie in a lie. Pigsy is captured. Silver Horn and Gold Horn use their five talismans against Monkey.

It was spring. The pilgrims had crossed the Country of Precious Ivory and were at the foot of yet another range of mountains. They met a woodcutter, who was actually a local guardian spirit in disguise, who warned:

"This is Peace Mountain, where the Cavern of Flowers is located. The names are pretty. The facts are not. The two monsters that live there have been waiting for you. They even hung a portrait of Tang Sung in their main hall to whet their appetite for his flesh. In the meantime, they have been eating every monk who tries to cross to the other side of the mountains. Their power is great because they possess five precious Talismans: the Lethal Vase; the Urn of Death; the Sword of Seven Stars; the Banana Leaf Fan; and the Gold Cord Which Can Subdue Dragons.

The "woodcutter" then disappeared in a puff of smoke. Naturally, Master, though petrified with terror, was still determined to continue. To give himself courage, he said,

"Well, that's a dire warning. But not only do we have Money King's powers to protect us, we also have Brother Chu (Pigsy) and Brother Sha (Sandy). With three of you, nothing can stop us."

In his heart, Monkey agreed perfectly with this, but he felt that he was doing too much work. It was time for that lazy layabout, Pigsy, to do more.

"Brother Pig," said Monkey in friendly tones, "indeed, I was wrong not to realize how very much you contribute to our voyage. Which would you rather do, guard our Master or act as advance scout for Peace Mountain?"

What Pigsy really preferred to do was to eat a big meal, drink a gallon of wine, and sleep on the baggage. However, he didn't want to lose face. He offered to be the advance scout. After all, the weather was mild, Peace Mountain was a very pretty mountain, and it would be much easier to take a nap once he was out of Brother Monkey's sight. So he leaped into the clouds and took off. Monkey, chuckling to himself, changed himself into a fly and followed.

Pigsy did try. For at least an hour, he diligently scoured the area and even checked behind all the rocks. But he soon was tired and said to himself:

"Brother Souen is certainly hyperactive. He never stops twitching and flitting about. Well, I'm made of steadier stuff. Why scout at all? Why not get a good night's rest and just march straight ahead? Even if I find a totally safe passage, Brother Monkey will get all the credit. Look, there's a nice shade tree near the rock. I've gone far enough. I will just report that we are on Stone Block Mountain, and it is inhabited by powerful monsters. And I will claim I beat off all those monsters and opened a safe passage for everyone. It's definitely nap time."

In moments, he was fast asleep under the tree. Monkey had heard every word. He flew back to camp and told Master exactly what Pigsy would say when he returned. So when Pigsy showed up and told his tale, Master lectured him about lying. Pigsy was so embarrassed that even his ears turned red. He promised to really scout the area, and he set out again. Still embarrassed, he kept thinking he saw Monkey in every bird, bug, and animal he passed.

Now the two masters of Peace Mountain were Silver Horn Monster and Gold Horn Monster. They had alerted all their monster servants to be on the lookout for any of the travelers. They had even showed them pictures of Master, Monkey, Pigsy, and Sandy to make sure they would recognize them. When Pigsy encountered thirty of their monster soldiers, he tried to pretend to be just another wandering monk who knew nothing of the pilgrims. But his huge ears and pig's snout looked exactly like the picture and they weren't fooled. Silver Horn immediately appeared to lead the attack on Pigsy. Outnumbered, Pigsy decided to flee, but tripped on a vine and was captured. The monsters put him in a pen and happily began arguing over whether he would taste better smoked, roasted, or stewed.

Silver Horn knew that Monkey King was too powerful to attack directly, so he decided on a ruse. He took the form of an elderly Tao doctor, covered with bleeding wounds. When Master saw this old man, lying in the path, he asked Monkey to carry him. Monkey could tell very well that this was a monster, but decided he'd carry him away from Master's sight before pulverizing him. After all, he had no desire to risk another argument with Master on the need to be compassionate or to get another skull-busting headache.

Unfortunately, Silver Horn guessed Monkey's plan. The minute they were around the bend, he said a special spell. Suddenly, Monkey was held down by the weight of three mountains. He frantically tried to free himself with his iron bar. Silver Horn returned to the campsite, defeated Sandy, and flew off with Master, Sandy, the Horse, and the baggage. To make absolutely sure of Monkey's defeat, Silver Horn gave his two most important generals, Subtle Phantom and Wise Serpent, two talismans—a red vase and a jade urn. They were to look for Monkey and, as soon as they saw him, to unplug both items, and call Monkey King by his real name Souen Wu Kung. When Monkey answered, he would be immediately sucked into the vase or the urn and be liquefied in minutes.

It took Monkey King almost half an hour to free himself. Once free, he returned to camp, only to find traces of a terrific fight that had uprooted trees and flung boulders about. He was now alone. He needed to use his brains. First, he went to the Celestial Emperor and asked him to order the local guardian spirits to help him. They should stay invisible but be ready to follow his instructions. And remembering that the local monsters would recognize him, he took the form of a Tao doctor. He soon met Subtle Phantom and Wise Serpent. He could tell they were carrying powerful talismans; the objects were surrounded by bright halos. When asked if he had seen a strange monk who looked just like a monkey, Monkey replied,

"Wait, I think so. Yes, I've heard of that monkey monk. Isn't he tremendously powerful? Didn't he even hold off Celestial troops? How can you possibly capture him?"

Serpent and Phantom were happy to have a chance to boast about their precious objects. The false Tao doctor didn't seem very impressed.

"That won't do the trick. Why, I have a treasure vase that is so large it can capture the sky. I'd be happy to lend it to you. If you want to borrow it, you can. I will just hold your treasures as a guarantee you will return it. Here, let me show you."

With this, Monkey transformed one of his hairs into a truly enormous vase. He threw it into the air, chanting,

"Now, Precious Vase, take the sky and keep it"

Immediately, the local guardian spirits used a "veil of darkness" to change day into night. Souen then chanted,

"Enough darkness, Precious Vase, let day shine."

The guardian spirits then removed the veil of darkness. The monsters were so impressed that they begged the false Tao doctor to trade their objects for his.

Once the exchange was made, the old "Tao doctor" appeared to leap into the sky and vanish. But with Monkey, appearances are often deceiving. Actually, Monkey had changed to the form of a cricket, and hid in Serpent's jacket. Now he undid his vase spell. The vase returned to his hide, becoming a hair again. The two monsters, dismayed over the loss of their precious objects, ran back to the cavern to tell Silver Horn of their failure.

However, Gold Horn and Silver Horn told them not to worry.

"We still have three precious objects left, the Sword of Seven Stars, the Banana Leaf Fan, and the Gold Cord Which Can Subdue Dragons. We are not going to wail about this. After all, we have the monk and two of his helpers. We even have a horse. We will celebrate our success, not our loss. We don't really care about Monkey."

They sent a Tiger Monster herald and a Lizard Monster herald to the cave of Gold Horn's mother to invite her to join them in feasting on Master, Pigsy and Sandy.

Monkey now transformed himself into a pretty young, woman monster, and joined Tiger Monster and Lizard Monster. Such a sweet thing, they thought. She was so charming that they were cajoled into telling her all about their errand, and the message they were carrying. Of course, Monkey killed them both as soon as he heard the story. Now he took the form of Lizard Monster, while he transformed one of his hairs into

Tiger Monster. Thus disguised, he went to the cavern of the Mother Monster. She was overjoyed at the invitation. She found her extra-sharp, meat-mincing dentures, got into a litter, and had her servants carry her off with the monster-heralds toward her son's abode.

After about six li on the route, Monkey killed the Mother Monster (whose corpse was that of a nine-tailed fox) and her litter-bearer monster servants. This time, he took her mother-form and changed four of his hairs into her servants. At the cavern, Gold Horn and Silver Horn greeted him warmly. He would have gotten away with his deception except that one of the monster-messengers ran to report that he had found the bodies of the heralds.

Hearing this, Gold Horn attacked Monkey with the Sword of Seven Stars, while Silver Horn held the Golden Cord. Gold Horn had no luck slashing at Monkey, since Monkey's flesh was even harder than supernatural seven-star metal. Monkey offered to let them all live if they would release Master, Pigsy, and Sandy. But Silver Horn threw the golden cord at Monkey. It looped around him, and knotted itself. It stayed tightly tied, no matter how small Monkey made himself. Delighted, Silver Horn grabbed back his precious Vase and Urn. He tried to cut off Monkey's head, first with a giant ax, then with a giant sword, then with a giant cleaver. Monkey's head refused to budge.

Silver Horn, busy chopping at Monkey, forgot to renew the "tie" magic spell on the Golden Cord, so Monkey was able to do one of his substitution tricks. He made one of his hairs into a fake monkey, made himself tiny, and slipped away. Next, he transformed himself into the shape of a Guard-Monster.

"Oh, Great Lord Silver Horn," he said, "that monkey monk you captured never stops wriggling. Since he has extraordinary powers, I am worried he will get away. May I have another strong cord to tie him more tightly?"

Silver Horn gave him another cord. Monkey snagged the real, magical Golden Cord, leaving the ordinary one in its place. Flying out of the cavern, he stopped at the entrance to challenge them.

Instead of rushing out to meet the challenge, Silver Horn unstoppered the vase, and said, "Enter, Souen Wu Kung."

Monkey could not stop himself from responding to his name. He found himself inside the vase, reduced to the size of a cricket. The vase was filled with powerful acid. A normal supernatural being would have been dissolved in no time. However, Monkey, who had even survived the Oven of Trigrams of the Great Immortal Tao Doctor, Lao Tze, had no problems. But he begged, and cried, and moaned for all he was worth. You can imagine how Master's heart ached for him. Pigsy and even Sandy began to weep for their lost Brother Monkey. Eventually all sounds from the vase ceased. An hour went by. Silver Horn decided it would be safe to open it. The minute he did, Monkey, in the form of a tiny mite, escaped.

Outside the cavern again, Monkey thundered out a challenge. Silver Horn and Gold Horn were now really furious.

"Will we ever get rid of this pesky Monkey Monk?" they thought. They charged out, ready to battle to the end, but they couldn't find him. Did he run away? Was he a coward after all?

No, but he had had an idea. Monkey waited until Silver Horn was alone. Taking the form of Gold Horn, Monkey joined him, saying he wanted to check the vase in case it had been damaged by that Monkey. He cautiously replaced it, not wanting to draw Silver Horn's attention, with a false vase that looked exactly like the real one. Now, Monkey called Silver Horn's name. Silver Horn responded, and was sucked into the vase, trapped, and liquefied. When Gold Horn returned and couldn't find his brother, he realized that somehow, Monkey must have tricked him.

Arming himself with the Banana Leaf Fan and the Sword of Seven Stars, he leaped into the clouds to fight Monkey. Monkey was ready. He had already transformed hundreds of his hairs into monkey-soldiers to fight the monster-soldiers. Gold Horn used the fan to create an enormous jet of flame and blasted the monkey-soldiers. Monkey (who had no fear of fire), just recalled all his hairs. He transformed one into an exact image of himself. This image then pretended to flee the flames. Gold Horn returned to his cavern, very pleased with himself, but so tired that he decided he would wait until the next day to eat Master, Pigsy, and Sandy. While he was sleeping, Monkey entered the cavern in the form of a servant-girl monster and stole the Banana Leaf Fan as well as the Magical Urn.

The next morning, Monkey challenged Gold Horn to single combat again. Gold Horn no longer had the Gold Cord, the Vase, the Urn, and the Banana Leaf Fan. He decided to run to seek help from his uncle the Great Fox King, who had ten times as many monster troops as he did. The minute that Gold Horn fled, Monkey ran into the cavern and freed Master, Pigsy, and Sandy. Master and Sandy were very grateful, but Pigsy was really annoyed that it took Monkey so long. His legs were all cramped and he was hungry. Furthermore, he really hadn't enjoyed listening to monsters arguing about cooking methods.

Monkey, Pigsy, and Sandy immediately set out for the Cavern of the Great Fox King. They attacked ferociously, fought all day and night, and killed Great Fox King. Monkey then called Gold Horn's name. When Gold Horn answered, he too was sucked into the Jade Urn and dissolved.

Monkey realized that the precious objects were so powerful that they must have been stolen from a Celestial Being. He took them up to Chang Ti. There, he learned that the objects had been owned by the Celestial Immortal Lao Kun. The Vase was a gourd he used for water, the Jade Urn was a sieve for his potions, the Sword of Seven Stars a stirrer for his pot, the Fan was used to fan the flames in the stove, and the Golden Cord was his belt. Silver Horn and Gold Horn were two dishonest servants, who had been tempted by the thought of making themselves kings. Now they had learned their lessons.

Opening the Vase and the Urn, Lau Kun recalled Silver Horn and Gold Horn to life.

He explained, "I allowed them to commit the theft. Without testing, they would never be able to face temptation. Without conquering temptation, they will never achieve sainthood."

Both Gold Horn and Silver Horn then knelt to Master, Monkey, Pigsy, and Sandy, and promised never to do evil again.

Chapter 21

Solving Earthly Problems

They meet with rude monks. Monkey shows his idea of diplomacy. The ghost of a king begs Master to help get the truth out about his murder and about an impostor acting as king.

Continuing on, they finally came to a great temple, the Temple of the Precious Forest. The impressive building was brightly colored, with enormous beams, marble floors, and beautifully carved stone statues. Master hastened to enter so that he could say special thanks in front of the statue of Kwan Yin. Now, the travelers had long since learned that it was wise to hide their best robes, their silver, and Master's special jeweled robes. Otherwise, they would just be telling local bandits whom to rob. So, though respectably clad, they wore plain cotton robes and were a bit dusty from the travel.

No sooner had Master crossed the threshold than a large, muscular monk, clad in rich silks, rudely ejected him, despite Master's attempts to explain who they were. Not only that, instead of offering them the hospitality of a temple, the gatekeepers told them:

"Off with you. The louse-ridden beds in the inn should be good enough for you beggar monks. Is there no end of you? You'd think every begging monk in the world wanted to travel here. Well, we have to take care of ourselves. What kind of good life would we have if we shared everything with you?"

Hearing this, Master had tears in his eyes. He was afraid to stay at an inn, but be was saddened at the thought of how far the temple monks had fallen from proper and holy behavior. Monkey suggested another approach.

"Well, Master, you won't get anywhere being holy and humble with this lot. There's only one way to deal with bullies like them."

At that, Monkey pulverized a few hundred-foot-tall trees and a two- or three-ton boulder just to show he was serious. Then, he yelled at the cowering monks. It was time to treat the Official Holy Monk of the Tang Empire, and his Honorable Disciples, the Great Brother Monkey King, the Great Pig Brother, and the Great Sand Monk like the very important people they were. Aware that they could either have their temple reduced to rubble or to welcome these visitors, the temple monks quickly got on their knees and invited them to stay.

That evening after a dinner that left even Pigsy feeling stuffed, Master and his disciples went into the temple gardens to enjoy the mild evening and look at the moonlight. They all missed their homes. Feeling nostalgic, they decided to go to bed early. In the middle of the night, Master dreamt that a man in a king's robe came to him, knelt, and said:

"I was once the King of Black Rooster Nation. Seven years ago, we had a terrible drought. I issued a proclamation promising eternal brotherhood to any Holy Man, Tao Doctor, or Great Sage who could end the drought and save my people. Many came, but they all failed. Then one day, a hermit, called Tsan Chen arrived. He used special incantations, and, the drought was over. He asked for no reward and lived the life of a Holy Man. We became blood brothers and the best of friends.

"One night three years ago, while we were walking in the garden, he tossed something into a well. It emitted a brilliant light. As I leaned over the edge of the well to look, he pushed me in. I have been dead for three years. Not only did I die, but no one even knows that I died, because he took my form. He has reigned as king ever since. As for the well, he had it closed and he planted a banana tree over it.

"Unable to rest, my spirit wandered in the Shadowlands, lamenting my fate. The day before your arrival, an underworld spirit guide told me that Tang Sung, a Holy Monk from the Tang Empire and his three disciples were destined to help me.

"I have a wife, the Queen, whom I love as my life, and a son, the Crown Prince He has been under house arrest ever since the evil hermit replaced me. He has also been forbidden to see his mother, who is under confinement in the queen's palace. They do not realize that it is not I who does this to them. You will meet my son tomorrow, as he always visits the temple after he goes hunting with the people who keep watch over him. Please tell him my story. I know he will act to free my kingdom from its evil ruler. Here is a jade scepter that you can use to convince the prince. I will also tell this to my queen in her dreams."

Then the spirit disappeared with a clap of thunder. Master awoke abruptly. He found a carved jade scepter at his bedside. So it had been a true vision and not just a dream. Master called his disciples together and asked them to help him meet the crown prince (who would, of course, be surrounded by his court and not easy to talk to alone). Monkey transformed one of his hairs into an elegant ebony wood box for the scepter. He would bring the prince to the temple, then make himself as small as a gnat and hide in the box. Monkey advised:

"Ignore the prince when he enters the temple. Don't come out to greet him. Just continue with your prayers. This is so disrespectful that he will want to scold you in person. As soon as he comes near you, show him the box."

At dawn, Monkey, leaving Pigsy and Sandy to guard Master, leaped into the clouds. When he saw black monster vapor hanging over the city, he knew for sure that their adversary was not an ordinary human magician. He also saw a hunting party in the forest near the temple.

After transforming himself into a large stag, he managed to lure the prince and the hunting party to the doors of the temple, then vanished. The prince took the disappearance of the stag to be an omen. Perhaps he should enter the temple and pray. He found a monk (Master) praying in front of the statue of Kwan Yin. The monk ignored him. Now, a prince, even a prince under house arrest, expects to be treated with great respect. In this situation, a monk should have knelt to the prince, then withdrawn in acknowledgement of the prince's superiority. But this one just continued with his prayers. Furious, the prince seized Tang Sung by the arms. Master addressed him calmly.

"Why should I make obeisance to you, you ungrateful and unfilial son?"

"What do you mean by that, wretched monk?" sneered the prince.

"Your father is dead. How can you live with yourself when you have done nothing to avenge him? You even call his murderer 'Father'. I am Tang Sung, a Holy Pilgrim sent from the Tang Empire to retrieve the True Scriptures from India. Last night, your Father's spirit spoke to me and told of his murder. If you have any filial piety at all, you will listen to his message."

The prince was so surprised that he collapsed.

"Can this be true?" he asked.

"Look in the ebony box," said Master. The prince yanked it open to see not only the scepter but a small monkey, dressed in human clothes.

Jumping out, the Monkey said: "I am the Monkey King, Great Saint Equal of Heaven, and a disciple of Tang Sung, the Holy Monk from the Tang Empire, whom I call Master. Like Master said, your father's spirit came to him last night and asked him to tell you the truth about his fate. He left the scepter behind as proof that this was a true vision."

The prince then told them another version of events three years ago.

"My father," he said, "was walking in the garden with Tsan Chen, the Great Hermit and my father's blood brother. A terrible wind carried off both Tsan Chen and the scepter. Since then my 'father' has continued to rule, but he became displeased with me and has kept me under guard. He and the queen seem to have also separated, and I haven't been allowed to see her."

The prince continued:

"I want to believe you. My father has been cold and distant to both my mother and to me. That is not like him. It is all very confusing. How can I be sure you are telling the truth, and are not some monster that took both Tsan Chen and the scepter?"

"Easy," said Monkey, "Take the scepter with you and find a way to sneak into the queen's place. When you see your mother, ask her if her relations with her husband have changed. Then, if you are convinced that we have told the truth, come back to the temple."

That night, the prince disguised himself as a palace sweeper. He drew no attention when he entered the queen's palace. Sweeping his way to a rubbish dump, he found the small hidden gate that opened on the queen's private garden. There he waited. Soon he heard her voice excusing her servants as she entered to sit in the garden alone, as was her custom during the full moon. The prince stepped out of the shadows to find her waiting expectantly. Her husband, she said, had come to her in a dream. He had told her to wait for her son in the garden. This made it much easier for the prince to tell her all that had happened. When he asked if her relations with the king had changed, she wept as she described how cold the king had become.

"Up to the day before the storm in which the Great Hermit disappeared, he was the most loving of husbands. Our hearts beat together. Our only wish was to live long together and die on the same day. Abruptly, he became cold and distant. He moved to the King's Palace and confined me to the Queen's Palace. Except for ceremonial occasions when my presence is required, he doesn't even speak to me."

This convinced the prince. He rode at a gallop back to the temple. Although Master and Monkey were ready to help, they still needed to convince the people that the king on the throne was an impostor.

"We need the king's body as final proof. We are going to have to get it out of that well," said Master.

Now, Monkey, although otherwise powerful and fearless, was uncomfortable in water, especially murky old wells. Maybe Pigsy was better suited, he thought. Besides, didn't Pigsy still owe him a bit for badmouthing him to the Master when they had met the White Bone Demon? But Pigsy never tried very hard unless food or treasure was involved. So, Monkey told Pigsy:

"Brother Pig, I am really upset. I could have recovered the famed Black Rooster Treasure. I understand hundreds of years ago a king had it dumped in a well to protect it from invaders. He then hid the well under a banana tree. One of the monks in the temple showed me where it was. But I really don't see too well in water, especially murky well water."

Treasure? Pigsy could hardly wait to jump in the well. As a former Celestial River Marshal, he was absolutely at home in water. Monkey lengthened his staff until it reached the bottom of the well and Pigsy climbed down. At the bottom, he found himself in an underground cavern with a small marble palace inscribed "Palace of Crystal, Domain of the Well Dragon." (In the Middle Kingdom, all the waters had dragon kings, even wells.) The dragon, recognizing Pigsy from his days as Marshal of the Celestial River, welcomed him with delight. But Pigsy was soon both suspicious and disappointed when the dragon, when asked about the well's treasure, described only a human body, perfectly preserved by the Magic Pearl of Preservation. So grumbling about sneaky monkeys, liar monkeys, and unfair brothers, Pigsy carried the body up from the well. He would find a way to get back at Monkey later.

When Master saw the body, he wept tears of pity. Pigsy, although likely to get tricked because of his greed, was rather intelligent. He had an idea.

"Dear Master, I'm so glad that I could help by bringing this unfortunate human back from the well. But it really was a pretty menial task. I'm just sorry that I can't bring him back to life. I know that would make you happy. Fortunately, Big Monkey Brother can easily do it."

"I can't do that, Master!" exclaimed Monkey.

"Oh yes he can," said Pigsy. "Just tighten the circle around his head. As soon as he feels that headache, he will come up with a way."

Monkey, remembering previous headaches, had no choice. Monkey did, in fact know that the king could be revived with a cinnabar pill. But to get one, he would have to go begging once again to the greatest Tao doctor of all, Lao Tze.

"Lao Tze still has probably not forgotten that incident when I had that terrible hangover," thought Monkey. "Did he even realize until then that those pills can cure hangovers as well as restore people to life? He should thank me."

But, no matter. He was going to have to apologize once more to Lao Tze, or face a permanent headache for disappointing Master. So Monkey vaulted up to heaven, swallowed his pride, paid up his apology debt to Lao Tze, and was able to beg one tiny cinnabar pill.

Once back, he lost no time in popping the cinnabar into the dead king's mouth. The pill worked instantly. The king began to breathe again. As he revived, they filled him in on events of the last three years and on their plan to redeem his kingdom. To keep him safe, they disguised the king as a monk and swore the temple monks to silence.

While Monkey had been with Lao Tze, Master had been equally busy reforming the temple monks. They had heard many sermons. Maybe the sermons converted them or perhaps they said anything in order to avoid more sermons. In any event, they all promised to reform their lazy, proud, and greedy ways.

In half a day's travel, Master, Monkey, Pigsy, Sandy, and the disguised king came to the capital. It was the custom in that country for anyone who wanted to right a wrong to ring a special gong outside the palace. Of course, Monkey rang it especially hard. They were brought into the chamber where the king held his audiences. The false king was not fooled, though, and recognized the true king despite his disguise. Just like that, he switched to the form of the Great Hermit, Tsan Chen, and leapt into the sky.

Monkey King leapt in pursuit, but Tsan Chen blew out such a dark cloud that even Monkey had trouble seeing through it. While Monkey was chasing the cloud, Tsan returned to the palace in the form of Master. When Monkey King returned, he saw two masters. He couldn't tell them apart. Tsan had created a black monster aura around both of them. Then, Monkey had an idea. He asked each one in turn to recite the "skull-busting headache" formula. As soon as he felt a terrible headache, he knew which was the real Master. He prepared to pulverize Tsan, but it took a moment for Master to remove the headache formula, and Monkey was slowed a bit. Tsan fled, with Pigsy and Sandy joining Monkey in full pursuit.

Just as they got close enough to kill him, they heard a voice calling them.

"Stop! Don't hit him."

The voice was so powerful and serious that even Monkey came to a screeching halt. Before them stood a Buddha, obviously one of the Lesser Buddhas who had reached a high level of perfection. His hand lay gently on the head of a large green lion. The Buddha spoke:

"It is my custom to come to earth regularly and to reward the pious. Three years ago I came down in the form of a poor beggar monk to personally reward the King of Black Rooster Nation for his pure life. But the king was irritated that a ragged monk would dare to insist on seeing him. He chained me in a pond for three days. I determined that he needed to be punished by lying in a well for three years. I ordered my mount, the Green Lion, to take his place as king for three years. During that time the kingdom has prospered. My hope is that the king will have learned a bit of humility.

So, Monkey, Pigsy, and Sandy returned to the palace and explained why the king had been drowned

"Things are not always what they seem," mulled Pigsy.

Monkey, although he didn't say it, thought about how he preferred straightforward battles with monsters. But, since the king was now alive again, everyone celebrated, with many promises of better and humbler behavior in the future. The king wanted to load the pilgrims with gifts. To Pigsy's disappointment, Master agreed to accept only a little rice. They should, he said, travel light, relying on the goodness of the people along their way.

Chapter 22

Red Child

The Red Child Monster fools the Master and kidnaps him during a sandstorm. Kwan Yin helps capture Red Child.

Autumn turned to winter. They all had to wear their heavy, quilted coats. When they came to a very steep mountain, Monkey noticed a red light shining from a large cavern. Concerned, he asked Pigsy and Sandy to guard Master while he took the form of a bird and flew to the cavern. A marble gate identified it as the Cavern of Clouds and Fire. A huge silk banner, embroidered with the words "Young and Saintly Great Red Child King" fluttered in front of the gate. This Red Child King was the son of a powerful monster. Red Child had read the stars and knew that Tang Sung would be coming with three powerful disciples. And, of course, he also wanted very much to gain immortality by eating Master's flesh. Knowing that Master, though very intelligent and holy, was also innocent and naive, Red Child took the form of a seven-year-old boy who was tied to a tree. As the travelers drew near, he began to cry and scream for help.

Master wanted to rush to the boy's aid, but Monkey spotted his noxious black monster aura. He, Pigsy, and Sandy formed a ring and prepared to defend Master. Realizing no one was coming to "help" him, Red Child leaped into the clouds, following them at a distance. When they stopped to camp before crossing their first mountain pass, he tried again to trick them, this time taking the form of an injured child. Master, who preferred to believe his own eyes rather than Monkey's warnings, ordered

Monkey, on pain of another skull-busting headache, to help.

Red Child, still pretending to be a scared little boy, told them he had been kidnapped by bandits who killed his entire family. He would be all right if they helped get him to his "uncle" who lived nearby. He refused to sit on the Horse or be carried by Pigsy or Sandy. Instead, he asked Monkey, the smallest disciple, to carry him. Pigsy and Sandy had decided that Monkey was overly suspicious, paranoid even. But Monkey could detect the monster's aura because his eyes were much sharper than theirs.

At being ordered to carry a monster, Monkey become so angry that he leaped into the clouds, shouting, "Well, if you trust him, you take care of him. I need a break from all these chores and your ingratitude."

The minute Monkey vanished, Red Child bounded into the clouds and raised a fierce sandstorm—fiercer than the winter sandstorms from the Gobi Desert. As the wind whipped the sand, blinding Pigsy and Sandy, Red Child grabbed Master and disappeared.

When Monkey cooled down enough to return he found the campsite completely wrecked and Pigsy and Sandy rubbing their sore eyes. They found no sign of Master. Monkey was so angry that he transformed himself into a three-headed, six-armed giant monkey and began to tear down the mountain. This brought the local mountain guardian spirits running. They had been hiding for a year after Red Child had defeated them. Hoping for help, they told Monkey all they knew about Red Child:

"Red Child is the son of Phantom King of Buffalos and of Princess Steel Fan. He possesses a terrible weapon, the True Fire, and no being is immune from it. Only the Steel Fan can extinguish that terrible, all-devouring, magic fire."

The mountain guardian spirits then showed them how to find the Cavern of Clouds and Fire again.

As they approached, Monkey King shouted, "Release my master or I'll pull the mountain down around your ears."

Red Child charged out, waving a lance tipped with fire. He and Monkey fought all morning, but finally Red Child felt himself weakening. Pigsy joined the fight, and Red Child pretended to flee into the cavern. But he turned, muttered a spell, and blew a jet of red flame at them both, so they had to flee. Back at their camp, Sandy suggested that they find something that would counter the fire. Perhaps, the Dragon King of the Eastern Sea would help. If they could lure Red Child out into in the open, the dragon, hiding in the clouds, could douse the flames with water.

So Monkey, Pigsy, and Sandy went to the Dragon King of Eastern Seas, who had long since forgiven Monkey for taking the iron staff from the bottom of his sea and for taking his dragon brothers' royal clothes. The Dragon King was happy to help. Monkey and Pigsy returned to the cavern and thundered out challenges to Red Child. They called him a coward, a baby who still smelled of his mother's milk, and a whining weakling. Red Child stormed out to fight, and blew a jet of flame at them. The Dragon King was waiting in a cloud, and released a torrent of water on Red Child. But the water just made Red Child's fire burn hotter. Worse yet, smoke blinded Monkey, and the magical fire entered his mouth and began to burn him from the inside. Monkey rolled on the ground in agonies and couldn't escape. Sandy tried to keep Monkey cool by heaping snow on him. Pigsy went in search for help from Kwan Yin.

But Red Child was very clever. He flew ahead of Pigsy and took the form of Kwan Yin. Fooled, Pigsy told her the whole story. The false Kwan Yin promised to help. Of course, when the two of them returned to the Cavern of Clouds of Flame, Red Child resumed his own shape and his monster soldiers tied up Pigsy. Sandy, hearing the monster soldiers cheer as they captured Pigsy, bravely challenged them to combat so that Monkey could escape to seek help. In minutes, Sandy was captured. Monkey was still too weak to charge in and fight, but he was able to change himself into a small green fly and fly into the cavern. While flitting around, he learned that Red Child had sent his six generals to invite his father and mother to a banquet so they could all enjoy eating Master's flesh.

Well, Red Child was not the only one who could transform himself. Monkey, in a flash, changed from a fly to the form of Red Child's father, the Phantom King of the Buffaloes. He transformed his hairs into the King's retainers and soldiers. The false "Phantom King" met up with the Red Child's six generals when they were half way to the Phantom King's palace. Of course, the generals were fooled, and brought him to the Cavern.

Greeting Red Child, the false Phantom King said:

"Dear Red Child, how good to see you. As your generals can tell you, I was on the way to your cavern already to give you some wonderful news. I have seen the light and decided to reform my evil ways. I will now be a vegetarian and urge you, my son, to do the same. If we use our power for good, we can achieve immortality the right way— by virtuous living."

Red Child, who knew his father just loved meat, especially human flesh, thought this was pretty suspicious. He decided to test his father.

"As a true son, I will always obey you. But before I do anything, I need to cast a horoscope. For that I need the exact moment of my birth. I can't seem to remember it. Can you tell me?"

Monkey, still in the father's shape, had no idea of the time of Red Child's birth. He could only pretend that old age prevented him from remembering.

Immediately, Red Child screamed, "Impostor! Seize him!"

Monkey had to flee. He flew all the way to Kwan Yin's Palace and begged her to help. She threw a vase into the Southern Sea. In moments, a huge, old tortoise returned with the vase, now full of the purest water from the deepest part of the sea. Kwan Yin then put a drop of the water on Monkey and healed all his burns. She flew with him to the cavern on a lotus leaf. Now Kwan Yin took the form a halo. She transformed thirty-six swords into a lotus throne in the sky. Again, Monkey challenged Red Child to combat. After the fifth round of fighting, he pretended to flee. Red Child, feeling victorious, spotted the lotus throne in the sky and decided to sit on it. The minute he did, the throne changed back into thirty-six swords, and trapped him. At the same time, Kwan Yin, resuming her shape, poured the magical water on him. That completely destroyed his ability to spew out fire. Red Child begged for mercy. He promised to fully reform, so Kwan Yin released him. But he tried to attack her again. This time, she took a gold bracelet from her arm and threw it into the air. It became five gold rings, which attached to him, painfully, at his wrists, ankles, and neck. She left, taking him with her. Eventually, she did reform him, but that is another story.

With Red Child out of the picture, Monkey King could now defeat the monster generals, chase away the monster soldiers, and free Master, Sandy, and Pigsy.

Chapter 23

Black River Monster

The Monster of the Black River opposes their passage.
A river guardian asks for justice.

After another month of travel, they came to the Black River, a great river with dark, inky water. Just as they realized they couldn't get Master across without building a boat, they saw a boatman arrive. His boat was very small, so only Master and Pigsy went on the first crossing. Before they reached the other side, a waterspout boiled up and enveloped the boat, Pigsy, and Master. In seconds, they had disappeared. Sandy, who had once been a river monster, offered to search. Under the black water, he found an enormous building, the Dwelling of the Spirit of Black Waters. Transforming himself into a minnow, he entered. A group of water monsters were discussing how to best cook Master and Pigsy. Half were in favor of boiling and the other half were for steaming them. Hearing this, Sandy resumed his usual form and challenged the head monster to combat. After about thirty bouts, Sandy pretended to weaken and he fled, trying to lure the monster to the shore where Monkey was waiting. But the monster was too smart to fall for this trick. Besides he had work to do, such as writing invitations to the feast.

Sandy and Monkey then called on the local river spirit. The spirit, creeping out of some reeds near the shore, said:

"I will be eternally grateful if you defeat this pernicious monster. The Dwelling of the Spirit of Black Waters was once my home but he expelled me from it. Since then, I have had to hide in the reeds. My cup is full of bitterness. I went to the Dragon King of the Western Seas and made a formal complaint against him. Alas, this Dragon King was his maternal uncle and refused to even listen to me."

Monkey decided to visit the Dragon King of the Western Seas and see if he could be more persuasive than a tired old river spirit. On the way to the Dragon King's palace, he saw a fish monster carrying a message box with a message for the Dragon King. Transforming himself into one of the Dragon King's soldiers, he grabbed the message box. The message said:

"I, True Crocodile, your nephew, ninth son of your younger sister, wish to announce the capture of Tang Sung and his disciple, Pigsy. You are hereby invited to feast on Tang Sung's flesh, one bite of which will grant you immortality. His pig disciple should make a gamey, but nice, side dish."

Still in the form of a Dragon King soldier, Monkey delivered the message. As the Dragon King was reading it, Monkey resumed his form and thundered:

"Corrupt and unworthy Dragon King! Consorting with monsters, preparing to eat human flesh, especially the flesh of a monk sent by Kwan Yin on a holy pilgrimage! The Celestial Emperor will hear of this! How dare you give special preference to your nephew and not punish him for displacing the Guardian Spirit of the Black Waters?"

The Dragon King was so scared that his scales almost fell off. Trembling, he knelt and said:

"Forgive me Great Saint Equal of Heaven. My younger sister is bitter because her father was decapitated by the Celestial Emperor, as punishment for disobeying Heaven in the amount of rain he sent. Her heart became hard. She taught her son my nephew badly and he turned to evil. You have reminded me of my duty as a Dragon King and I will gladly help you,"

The Dragon King ordered True Crocodile to release Master and Pigsy. True Crocodile refused and attacked, but was defeated and made to return to the Dragon King's realm. The Guardian of the Black River reclaimed his home. In gratitude, he parted the waters of the river so that Master and his disciples could cross to the other bank.

CHAPTER 24

Buddhists and Taoists

The travelers meet monks pushing a cart and learn that Buddhists are persecuted for failing to end a drought, while three Tao Immortals and all Taoists are given preference. In the Temple of the Three Pure Ones, Great Saint adds to his renown. Monkey King and Master engage in a contest of powers with the Ram Immortal, the Deer Immortal, and the Tiger Immortal. The King recognizes his injustice and the Buddhists are restored to their temples.

So the pilgrims continued until, in April, they reached the nation of Chou. While approaching a town they heard a loud rumbling on the road behind them. Monkey leaped into the clouds, but instead of monster auras, he saw a group of very thin, raggedly dressed monks pulling a large cart loaded with tiles, beams, and bricks. The old, noisy cart was heavy, and the monks barely inched along. Two well-fed Taoist doctors, dressed in silk robes, were using whips to make them move faster. Monkey had heard of this country, where Buddhists were despised and Taoists and Tao doctors had all the wealth and power. To learn more, Monkey took the form of a fat and happy-looking Tao doctor, introducing himself as a traveler looking for a place to stay. One of the Tao doctors welcomed him.

"In the country of Chou, no Tao doctor or practitioner of Taoism need ever beg his rice. The King hates Buddhists and has given them to us as slaves so that we will have more workers when we build larger temples."

"How did this happen?" asked the false Tao doctor. "In the Middle Kingdom, both Buddhism and Taoism are respected, but neither controls the other. The Tang Emperor is a Buddhist but respects all creeds that teach people to do good rather than evil."

"There's good reason for our King's preference," responded the Tao Doctor. "Twenty years ago, the kingdom suffered a terrible drought. All the prayers of the people and Buddhist monks were to no avail. Then suddenly three Tao Immortals, the Tiger Immortal, the Deer Immortal and the Ram Immortal, came from Heaven. They brought us rain and abundant harvests. Because of their failure, Buddhist monks were given to us as slaves."

Monkey, still as the false Tao doctor, then asked the monks if any of them knew the fate of his uncle, a Buddhist monk named True Way. None had heard of his uncle, but they thought True Way was probably enslaved like they were, or dead. No one dared to escape. Many older monks had already died from ill treatment. They clung to hope only because of a prophecy that they would be liberated by a monk from the Middle Kingdom and his disciples. Resuming his true form, Monkey ordered the two Tao doctors to free these innocents. When they refused, he tossed the doctors and the cart into a ravine. He gave one of his hairs to each of the freed monks so that they could call him if they needed. The monks directed them to a ruined temple where Master could hide and rest.

At the ruins of the Temple of Prudence, they were welcomed by a few vagrant monks who had escaped capture. Monkey, Pigsy, and Sandy went out that night to the Taoist Temple of the Three Pure Ones, to see what they could learn about the Tiger, Deer, and Ram Immortals, who were hosting a banquet. This temple was dedicated to three very famous Taoist Immortals, Lao Tze, Sha Jeng, and Ling Pao. Their statues stood by the altar. Monkey used a spell to raise such a storm that all the Taoists, even the Immortals, fled. In case anyone saw them, Monkey, Pigsy, and Sandy each took the form of one of the three statues of the famous Taoist Immortals. They feasted to their heart's content. They ate so much that even Pigsy was stuffed, and were settling down to a nap. Suddenly, a sneeze! One of the little Taoist disciples had been hiding under the table. He rushed out in a frenzy, eager to tell the other Taoists that the statues of the Three Immortals had come to life and feasted. Monkey, Pigsy, and Sandy decided to remain in statue form to see what would happen. When the Tiger, Deer, and Ram Immortals returned with the little disciple, they decided a miracle had occurred. Clearly, the statues had come to life to show their appreciation for how much the Tiger, Deer, and Ram Immortals had done for the Taoists in the kingdom. So they began to chant and pray. They begged the statues for some celestial elixirs to extend their lives.

Monkey couldn't resist this opportunity for a great Monkey-style practical joke. In his living-statue mode, he confirmed that indeed, they had come down from the Celestial Realms to show their appreciation. They would be happy to provide some elixir, but no one must look as they prepared the secret formula. Pigsy, Sandy, and Monkey then each took a gold ceremonial cup and pissed into it. The cups were presented to the Three Immortals. Whew! The Immortals were surprised to find that the celestial elixir really stank. The Tiger Immortal said his smelled like monkey urine. The Deer Immortal said his smelled just like pig urine, and the Ram Immortal said his could be best described as "rotten fish-y." Still, they drained their cups.

Monkey, Pigsy, and Sandy then reverted to their true shapes, laughing hysterically. They leaped into the sky and vanished, leaving behind three humiliated, furious Tao doctors.

The next day, when Master and his three disciples presented their credentials to the King and his advisors, the three Tao doctors recognized Monkey, Pigsy, and Sandy as the malicious jokesters from the night before. They begged the king to kill these evil Buddhist monks. The King was just about to give the order but a delegation of provincial governors begged him not to do anything rash. The governors had come to report signs of a terrible drought. Another Drought-Ending Contest was needed.

What a challenge. It was too good to pass up. So Monkey, speaking for all of them, informed the King he had been fooled by monsters in the form of Tao doctors. Only the Master and his disciples were the true Holy Ones.

"In that case," said the King, "prove it by making it rain. You and the Tiger Immortal, the Deer Immortal, and the Ram Immortal will have a contest. The winners and their religion will be favored hereafter in my kingdom."

The Tiger Immortal went first. He took out his magical tablet. Normally he would strike it once and there would be wind; twice, and there would be clouds; three times and there would be lightning; four times and there would be rain. On the fifth tap, the clouds would be dispersed and rain would stop. He struck it once. The wind began to blow. But Monkey transformed a hair into an image of himself. Leaving the image behind, he changed into a bird and flew into the heavens. There he saw the guardian spirits of the air, who were busy responding to Tiger Immortal's magic tablet. Monkey threatened to pulverize them if they didn't help him. Naturally, they helped. So the wind died down.

Tiger Immortal struck the tablet again, but Monkey, still in the sky, persuaded the cloud guardian spirits to leave, so no clouds formed. So it went for three and four strikes. Now Monkey gathered together the wind, cloud, and thunder spirits, and the Rain Dragon, and instructed them to obey his signals. One wave of the staff for wind; the second for clouds; the third for lightning; the fourth for rain; and, the fifth, disperse. Then Monkey returned and took the place of his hair. He said:

"Your tablet doesn't seem to be in the mood to help today. My Master's prayers are always effective because he is truly good and holy."

Master began to pray and Monkey discretely waved his staff. The wind began to blow. With a second wave, thick clouds gathered. A third wave was followed by thunder and lightning. Rain fell at the fourth wave and at the fifth, the sun shone again.

The Immortals immediately claimed that it was their magic, not Master's prayers, that brought the rain. It was just that the presence of the ugly disciples had slowed the response time. Monkey laughed. He dared them to call the guardian spirits and the Rain Dragon to appear. They called and called, but there was no one.

Then Monkey whispered: "Come brothers, it's time," and the sky was filled with spirits and one enormous Rain Dragon.

The Tao doctors insisted on another duel of magic. The first contest was to see who could sit the longest in a lotus position on top of a column. Now, this was hard. Monkey was the weakest at sitting still, despite his supernatural powers. Pigsy was no better. Sandy wasn't very strong on sitting and meditating either. Monkey confided his worry to Master, who said:

"Your powers are without compare, Brother Monkey, but I have been trained in meditation since I was a little boy. If you can transport me to the top of the column, I can best the Tao doctor in meditation."

So it was done. Monkey turned another hair into an image of himself. He transformed himself into a bright halo which lifted Master to the top of the column. The Tiger Immortal decided to cheat and sent a hornet to sting Master. But Monkey saw it in time and blew it away.

"Two can play," thought Monkey. And he transformed himself into a scorpion, crawled under the Immortal's robes and stung him so hard that he fell off the column. Master was clearly the winner.

Deer Immortal then challenged them to a "Guess the Hidden Object" contest. The one who could describe correctly an object sealed in a box would be the winner. Monkey reduced himself to the size of a mite. He crawled through the keyhole into the box where he saw a tunic embroidered with the words "Tunic of Earth and Grain," and a robe embroidered with the words "Robe of Heaven and Earth." Monkey guessed that the Deer Immortal had chosen these garments for the king to put in the box. He transformed the garments into a broken bell and a broken clapper. Then he flew to Master in the form of a gnat.

"Say 'broken bell and broken clapper' when asked," he whispered.

Deer Immortal took his turn.

"I can see an embroidered tunic, the Tunic of Earth and Grain, and an embroidered robe, with the words 'Robe of Heaven and Earth' on it."

Master, in his turn, said, "There is a broken bell and a broken clapper in the box."

The king was ready to immediately behead Master for guessing wrong, but Monkey dared him to prove it by opening the box. The king and the Deer Immortal were utterly mystified by what they found. The Deer Immortal accused Master of black magic and insisted on a second trial. This time, only the king knew what was in the box. He had picked a peach and put it in himself. In the form of an insect, Monkey flew into the box, ate the peach and left the peach pit. Once again, he told Master, and once again, Master guessed correctly.

The Tiger Immortal begged for one more chance. This time, he hid two Taoist disciples in a locked closet. Monkey, once again sneaking into the closet, appeared in the form of a tiger monster. He threatened to eat the disciples unless they allowed him to shave their heads and to change their clothes into Buddhist robes. He told them they would also be eaten unless they came out only when they heard a voice call for Buddhist monks. Terrified, the two young disciples agreed.

The Deer Immortal guessed "two Taoist disciples" and called for them to come out. Nothing happened.

Then Master called, "Buddhist monks, come out."

They did, of course, to the total mystification of the king and Immortals.

Not ones to give up easily, the Immortals claimed that it was all trickery. The Tiger Immortal announced one final, infallible test. He was sure only he could pass it. It was safe from all dark magic. This test required each of them to reattach his decapitated head.

Monkey agreed and insisted that they also throw his head as far away as they could. He stood there calmly. In one quick swing, the executioner cut off his head, but there was no blood at all.

Although the Tiger Immortal sent an eagle to fly away with Monkey's head, Monkey's head shouted, "Time to rejoin head and body," and the eagle politely brought his head back. Monkey reattached his head. Now it was Tiger Immortal's turn.

The executioner's ax struck. The Tiger Immortal's head fell. Again there was no blood. Monkey knew that this no-blood spell would not hold if the head was moved too far away from the body. He changed one of his hairs into a yellow dog. The dog ran off with the head and jumped in the river. The Tiger Immortal's blood began to flow and he died, leaving behind the corpse of a beheaded tiger. It was clear to all that he had been a tiger monster, not a Tao Immortal, and he had used his powers to obtain a lot of monks to eat.

Deer Immortal wanted to avenge Tiger Immortal. He challenged Monkey to the "Reclosing the Wound" contest. In this test, Deer Immortal offered to let someone take out his innards. After they were put back in, he would close the wound.

"Great," said Monkey, "it'll help my digestion."

So he and Deer Immortal were cut open. Amazingly, there was no mess and no blood. Monkey tossed his innards around, jumped rope with his intestines, put them back, and closed himself up again. Deer Immortal tried to do the same. When he tried the jump-rope trick, he stumbled and the spell ended. He bled and died, leaving behind the carcass of a white deer, a deer monster that too had eaten many Buddhist monks.

The Ram Immortal insisted on the Test of Boiling. Monkey was delighted as his fur had gotten really dry and dull-looking after so much travel. By now, Pigsy was taking Monkey's victories for granted, and paying far more attention to the candies he was eating. So Monkey decided to give him a scare. When he jumped in the boiling oil, he changed himself into such a small nail that he seemed to disappear. The Ram Immortal then claimed victory because obviously Monkey had dissolved. Master cried with sadness, but Pigsy merely felt irritated that Monkey should have let them down this way. Monkey got so annoyed at Pigsy's complaints that he jumped out of the oil again.

Watching the Ram Immortal carefully, Monkey saw him toss something in the oil before he took his turn jumping into the cauldron. Changing himself back into a nail, Monkey tumbled to the bottom of the oil where he now saw a magic talisman, a Pearl of Coldness. Changing into a tiny monkey, he grabbed the Pearl and jumped out. No one saw him, but the oil began to really boil, and it cooked the Ram Immortal through and through. All that remained was the corpse of a giant ram.

The King realized that he had been under the influence of evil monsters. He had been unjust in suppressing the Buddhist monks, who had never done any harm and had tried do good. From then on, all religions that taught people to be better would be welcomed in his country. The surviving monks were invited to reclaim their temple. Before our travelers left the country, they all had a grand vegetarian feast.

CHAPTER 25

The Demon

The River at the Junction of Heaven stops the travelers. A villager tells them of the sacrifice of a boy and a girl to the Demon King. Monkey and Pigsy take the place of the boy and girl.

How fast the seasons passed. It was autumn again. They came to a vast lake, marked by a marble monument on which were carved the words "Salt Lake of the Junction of Heaven, 80 Li Wide. Never Crossed by any Human."

They searched the shore in vain for a boat. Finally they reached a village where they met a devout Buddhist named Jen Lee. Though the whole village was decorated as if for a great holiday, everyone was walking around with long faces. In fact their host could barely keep from crying. Master, who was gentle and kind, was finally able to persuade him to talk.

"Oh, Holy Monk, my heart is heavy because it is the time of year when we must give the Demon King Ling Kan one of our handsomest boys and our loveliest girls. It is true he protects the village from floods, but the price is terribly high. We tried not giving up our children, but he caused such terrible storms that many more people were killed. This year, it is my son and my best friend's daughter who lost the lottery and who are to be given as sacrifices."

Master and his disciples were deeply moved. Monkey offered to go in the boy's stead. Pigsy would then go in the girl's stead. While Monkey was able to turn himself into an exact image of the boy in no time, Pigsy had more of a problem. Though he could take many shapes, they all had some of his characteristics. For example, when he turned into an old man, he was always a fat, big, dark, hairy old man. When he turned into a young man, he became a large, heavy-set, coarse-looking young man. When he turned into a woman, he always turned into a large, piggy-looking female with an enormous behind. So his first version of the daughter was an ugly, fat girl, with a piggy-looking mouth. This would never fool the monster. He tried harder, but at best, he only managed a pretty head on a huge porky body. So Monkey had to help. His magic successfully transformed Pigsy into the very image of a lovely young girl.

The real children were carefully hidden in the cellar. Both Monkey (as the boy) and Pigsy (as the girl) lay down on a large red lacquer plate and waited patiently for the demon to come for them. Monkey reassured Pigsy:

"Don't worry, Brother Pig. You may look like a really tender and juicy little girl, but traditionally ogres, demons, and monsters start with the boys."

It grew very dark. Suddenly there was a great wind and the Demon King Ling Kan appeared before them. He was used to seeing the children sob with fear or just faint and so was really surprised to see the boy waiting so calmly. Suspicious, he announced that contrary to usual practice, he would eat the girl first. Hearing that, Pigsy decided he had helped out quite enough, and he resumed his true form. So did Monkey. Pigsy, armed with his giant steel rake, and Monkey, swinging his staff, then attacked Ling Kan. Not expecting any trouble, Ling Kan wasn't even carrying his best weapons. He decided to run away and fight another day. He fled in such a hurry that he left his chainmail armor behind. Because the chain mail was made of steel-hard fish scales, it was clear that he was some kind of marine monster.

Back at his court, Ling Kan told of his disaster. He was particularly upset that he would not be able to taste even a mouthful of Master's flesh. A wily perch general advised him that he could still succeed. If he froze the lake, then lured the travelers onto it, he could capture Master as soon as the travelers reached the lake's middle. Using his magic powers, Ling Kan caused the north wind to blow so fiercely for the next three days that the lake froze. The ice was more than three feet thick. To make it seem even safer, the Demon King sent his servants, disguised as travelers, onto the lake.

When the sun finally shone, Master and his disciples were delighted at their good luck. The lake was frozen. They could see dozens of travelers happily crossing the lake, and other people just skating and sledding. Pigsy, Monkey, and Sandy tested the ice and found it as hard as stone. Wrapping the Horse's hooves in straw, they then set out. Monkey was the only one who felt that the deep freeze was a bit too much of a lucky coincidence. But they traveled for a day and a night with no problems, and reached the middle of the lake.

Suddenly the ice cracked. Master disappeared. Taking the Horse and baggage to the other shore, Monkey, Pigsy, and Sandy searched frantically for Master. They knew that it was no winter accident but some kind of foul magic used to trap Master. Monkey, who was least comfortable in the water, would act as scout. Pigsy and Sandy prepared for water combat.

While they searched, Pigsy was given the task of carrying Monkey. Knowing that Pigsy wouldn't mind teaching him a lesson or two, Monkey actually transformed himself into a flea that sat on Pigsy's ear, while he let one of his hairs (wearing his shape) sit on Pigsy's shoulders. Good thing too, because after about a mile or so of complaining about Monkey's bossiness and his weight, Pigsy managed to fake a stumble so that he could heave Monkey into the water. Of course, the hair-Monkey disappeared and the "flea" on Pigsy's ear gave him a good strong "flea bite." This convinced Pigsy to avoid future water "accidents."

They searched until dark. Seeing a light in the depths, they dove down to an underwater palace, the Palace of the Sea Tortoise. Taking the form of a lobster soldier, Monkey entered the palace and persuaded the flounder kitchen maids to gossip. He learned that the Demon King intended to eat Master the next day. Although he could have eaten Master raw, he decided proper cooking would be more enjoyable. So the chef was making preparations and gathering special spices. Monkey soon found the air-bubble cage where Master was confined. Changing himself into a tiny insect, Monkey flew into Master's ear and whispered:

"Don't worry, Master, it is I, Monkey, in the form of an insect in your ear. Brother Pig and Brother Sand Monk are busy sharpening their weapons. We will certainly save you. Our plan is to have Brother Pig and

Brother Sand Monk challenge him to combat. Then they will pretend weakness and flee toward land. As soon as the monster comes to land, I will be waiting to engage him in combat."

It almost worked. Pigsy and Sandy came right to the palace, knocked down the gate and subdued the guards. They called Ling Kan a coward, a fool, an oppressor of the innocent, and other, even worse, names. The angry demon attacked both Pigsy and Sandy. He chased them all the way to the shore, but dove back into the water the minute that Monkey leaped out of the clouds.

Pigsy and Sandy tried again. They came to his gates and insulted him, but he refused to come out. He remembered the old adage that "battles are also won by those with cool heads and the ability to outwait their enemies." So he decided to concentrate on preparing for the feast, featuring garlic-onion-anise-steamed Master as the main course, with kelp and sea cucumber side dishes.

Monkey was afraid that if he joined Pigsy and Sandy at the gates, it would only persuade the monster to eat Master raw. So he flew to Kwan Yin's palace again. She had already woven a small bamboo cage in preparation. Returning with him, she tossed the cage into the water, calling out,

"May a celestial goldfish enter. All others stay out."

In moments, the trap resurfaced, holding a large, beautiful goldfish. Once it had lived in Kwan Yin's goldfish pond. It had been washed to earth during a flood, and, enjoying its earthly freedoms, become the demon king. With their fish leader now recaptured, all the fish, shrimp, and lobster monsters fled. The villagers would not be troubled by floods again. Pigsy and Sandy retrieved Master. Thanking Kwan Yin, the voyagers returned to the village and shared in an enormous thanksgiving feast.

After the feast, a very large turtle came to shore. The original owner of the underwater palace, who had been ejected by the monster, the turtle gratefully carried the voyagers across the lake. He was highly interested to hear of Master's journey, and, in fact, had a request. He had lived as a turtle for many centuries, always trying to carry out good deeds. When, he wondered, would he be rewarded by rebirth as a human? Master promised to find out.

Chapter 26

Blue Buffalo

Master, Pigsy, and Sandy are captured by the Blue Buffalo Monster. Monkey King is disarmed in combat.

Winter had come again. They had left the gentle pasturelands behind and were once again faced with a mountain range. The route through the wild, desolate, and rocky land seemed to go on forever. Finally, they saw a large deserted temple ahead. Monkey warned them to be careful because he saw traces of black, noxious monster vapor. As was their custom on such occasions, Monkey traced a magic circle with his staff around Master, the Horse, Pigsy, and Sandy and warned them to stay inside while he scouted ahead and looked for food.

The area was deserted. Monkey finally found a woodsman's hut. When he knocked to beg food, the woodsman screamed in terror at the red-eyed, upright, walking, talking monkey at his door. It took Monkey quite a while to explain who he was. Since he spoke very politely, he was able to finally persuade the woodsman to give him rice and salted pickles for Master. He could have just knocked down the door and taken anything he wanted, but he didn't want to go against Master's instructions to treat all the people they met with courtesy.

He had taken so long that Master had become impatient waiting. The night wind was cold and the building looked quite deserted and harmless. Master ordered Pigsy and Sandy to go with him to seek shelter in the building. They found the building empty except for four embroidered tunics.

"Look, Master, obviously these tunics were left here just for us," Pigsy said. "You can tell that one will fit you perfectly. One looks like it was tailored for Brother Sandy, one looks right for Brother Monkey, and one looks just my size. It's cold and it certainly won't hurt to have another layer. Our clothes are beginning to look very tatty. We now look more like starving mendicant monks than honored envoys of the Tang Emperor."

Master refused to wear one, but Pigsy and Sandy donned theirs. Immediately, the tunics tightened, the arms and legs stuck to the sides, and they were trapped inside. As Master was frantically trying to cut the tunics off of them, a monster descended from a black cloud and carried all of them to his palace. He was very disappointed not to have captured Monkey as well with his tunic-trap.

Monkey returned, saw the empty circle, and followed their trail to the temple. Their baggage was in the corner, but there was no sign of them. With his superior vision, Monkey could follow the monster's vapor trail to an enormous cavern at the top of the mountain. "Gold Helmet Cavern, Home of the Great Buffalo King," stated the carved sign. Monkey shouted a challenge so loudly that rockfalls and avalanches crashed all around the cavern. The monster came out. They fought for hours. They were evenly matched, and neither gained an inch. Finally, the monster took a white jade bracelet from his arm and tossed it onto Monkey's iron staff, capturing the staff. Now disarmed, Monkey had to flee.

Monkey King had never fought a terrestrial monster with such powers. This could be only a being with an origin in the stars. It was time to ask the Celestial Emperor for help. Though Chang Ti, the Celestial Emperor, was unable to identify the stellar origin of the monster, he decided to order four of his chief officers to help Monkey. Two were generals with three heads and six arms, each armed with a sword, cord, and a mace. The other two were thunder dukes and controlled the power of both fire and water. The two generals fought the monster almost to a standstill, but finally the white jade bracelet disarmed both of them. The two Dukes of Thunder hurled lightning, fire, and water at the monster, but with no better success. The bracelet disarmed them as well. Even without his iron staff, Monkey King was a formidable fighter. He transformed his hairs into an army of monkeys who attacked again and again, but with no better success.

"If force and weapons don't succeed, I'd better rely on my talents as a thief. It's time to use my wits and not just rely on force," thought Monkey.

He entered the cavern in the shape of a green fly. Once inside, he took the shape of a small wolf-headed servant monster and searched the cavern until he found the strongbox where his iron staff was hidden. He reduced his size until he was small enough to pass through the key hole. Once inside, he transformed the staff into such a small pin that it fit in his ear cavity. He left one of his hairs behind in the form of his iron staff. Then he crept out of the strongbox, took the form of a small wolf-headed servant again and continued his reconnaissance. Fortunately, the cavern was packed with monsters, all scurrying back and forth, doing whatever busy monsters do, and no one noticed him.

Monkey waited until late evening before going to Buffalo Monster's quarters. He observed the monster getting ready to sleep and putting his precious jade bracelet onto his wrist for safekeeping. Monkey immediately transformed himself into a bed louse, crawled onto the bed and bit the monster's wrist just under the bracelet. No luck. The monster snored happily on. So Monkey set the room on fire. The monster woke up but was able to put out the fire using his magic bracelet. He was now also fully alert.

The Celestial Emperor sent more generals to help Monkey, but they, too, were all disarmed by the monster. It was time to go to a higher authority.

Monkey went all the way to Buddha's Gate, to the Guardians, known as the Lo Han. The Lo Han were equipped with special paralyzing grains of cinnabar. They gave their entire supply to Monkey. The cinnabar had never failed. But this monster just used his bracelet to take the cinnabar grains. Monkey decided to ask Lao Tze, the Celestial Tao Doctor, for more cinnabar to replace what the Lo Han had lost. When he arrived at Lao Tze's residence, usually a quiet, calm place, full of disciples busily preparing special elixirs, pills, and essences, he instead found groups of disciples running around frantically. Apparently, Lao Tze's Blue Buffalo had escaped while its herder was taking a nap. Now, Monkey realized the origins of the Buffalo Monster. He told Lao Tze the whole story and begged him to help.

Monkey returned to the cavern and thundered out another challenge:

"It is I, Great Saint Equal of Heaven, here to challenge you, you cowardly beast. You have no real powers or courage. How could you? You rely on a piece of jewelry to disarm your opponents. Without it, you would be less than nothing."

He called the monster even worse names. Finally, the monster lost his temper.

"That cursed Monkey is making so much noise, he'll ruin my appetite. How can I instruct the chef to cook Tang Sung, Pigsy, and Sandy properly? He's so loud, I can't even think."

So, he leaped out of the cavern and charged at Monkey with an enormous sword. Monkey pretended to flee into the clouds. As the Buffalo Monster mounted higher in the sky, he heard Lao Tze's voice calling him back. From high above, Monkey watched. Feeling the breeze from Lao Tze's magic fan and hearing his voice, Buffalo Monster transformed into a large, blue buffalo, his real shape. The Jade Bracelet resumed its function as his nose ring.

It seems that the Blue Buffalo was not evil, but after he escaped and descended from Heaven, he fell into a cavern full of monsters that had terrorized the area for decades. He had been elected their king, and not knowing any better, learned all their monster habits. (Evil companions will always lead one to evil.)

Now, Monkey was able to free Master, Pigsy, and Sandy. Then Monkey, Pigsy, and Sandy killed all the monsters that infested the cavern and freed the region from its evil.

CHAPTER 27

The Country of Women

They arrive at the Country of Women, where Master and Pigsy drink the water of the River of Fecundity and become pregnant. An old woman teaches them the use of the Water of Reversal.

It was now spring. They came to yet another river, where they saw an old, but strong-looking, white-haired woman poling a barge. That was odd. Big cargo barges are poled by men, while women pole the lighter house-boats. They were terribly thirsty. Master and Pigsy scooped up some river water in a gourd and drank it. Within half an hour, both had terrible stomach aches and their bellies began to swell. Both soon looked like pregnant women. Fortunately, by then they had come to a small town and could ask for help.

This was the Country of Women. There were no men. A female innkeeper told them that the river was called the "River of Fecundity" and any woman who wished to become a mother could drink from it. No man had ever drunk the river water. As a man cannot carry a baby, the water would probably only make the belly swell until it exploded. If a woman was too old, or not strong enough to carry a child, or a female child drank the water by accident, water from the "Well of Reversal" would reverse the effects of the river water. That was Master and Pigsy's only hope.

Unfortunately, a greedy Immortal called Ju Yi controlled the Well of Reversal. Monkey politely approached Ju Yi and begged him for a few drops of the magic water to save Master and Pigsy's lives. This Ju Yi was the uncle of Red Child, whom Monkey had defeated in battle. Ju Yi demanded an exorbitant fee before he would give them even one drop. After a long argument and a fight, during which Monkey couldn't both fight and fill his pail with well water, they both retired from the field to rest. The next day Monkey came back with Sandy and a plan. While Monkey fought Ju Yi, Sandy could dip into the well. Sandy succeeded in bringing up one small gourd of the magic water. Master and Pigsy drank the water and were delighted to resume their original shapes. They also learned that pregnancy for women was no easy matter. If labor pains were anything like what they suffered, it was amazing any female survived giving birth.

The next day, they continued to cross the Country of Women. Huge crowds followed them at every turn. Though the women had heard of men, and some had even seen paintings of men, this was the first time many had seen a real one. One look at Pigsy, Sandy, or Monkey was enough to persuade them that if these creatures were men, well, they weren't interested. But Master was handsome and well spoken. Many wished there were thousands like him in their kingdom.

Finally, they reached the capital of the country, and went to the palace to present their credentials and greetings from the Tang Emperor. The female King was overjoyed to see them and immediately offered to make Master her consort, who would rule by her side. Master was totally abashed and didn't know how to refuse her politely. He persuaded her to let him return to his friends to think over the offer. The next morning, she sent her female soldiers to hear his answer. Pigsy, acting as Master's spokesman, explained that they were monks and had vowed never to marry. Master couldn't say yes. Furthermore, they had not yet accomplished their mission. The King's messengers responded:

"Our noble king has anticipated your answer. She will give you all the help that she can for the pilgrimage, provided Tang Sung stays behind and lives as her husband. The disciples can go in his place and finish the mission."

To Master's horror, Monkey spoke up at this point:

"We thank you for this most reasonable offer and will indeed do so."

Delighted, the messengers left.

"Evil, treacherous monkey brain!" stormed Master. "How can you betray me this way?"

Monkey then explained that if Master didn't want Monkey to have to kill the king, her court, and about ten thousand of her soldiers getting Master out of this country, he'd better accept this little white lie.

"If we pretend to agree, she will grant your every wish. Just ask for permission to accompany us to the border. Once we're near the border, I will use my spell-that-fixes. That's the one that worked so well even on Celestial handmaidens and allowed me to steal the peaches from the Celestial Gardens. The guards will be rooted to the spot, and I'll release them when we're a day's journey beyond the borders."

The King personally escorted them to the engagement feast. She was a beautiful woman and Master looked perfect next to her. She agreed to let Tang Sung accompany his disciples to the border to say good-bye. But before Monkey even had a chance to say his fix-in-place spell, a sudden cyclone whirled the dust so high that everyone was blinded. While they were trying to pry open their eyelids, an unknown female seized Master and vanished.

The King and her retainers believed the dust storm to have been divine intervention, forbidding them to force a monk into marriage. Ashamed, they returned quietly to the capital. But where was Master?

Monkey, Pigsy, and Sandy flew into the sky and followed the dust storm all the way to a distant mountain, where they saw the storm enter yet another cavern, whose sign proclaimed, "The Cavern of Musical Winds." Taking the form of a bee, Monkey entered the cavern, where he saw a beautiful woman monster and her female soldier-monsters. Master was in a corner, eyes closed, mumbling prayers. The female monster cooed to him:

"Even here in these mountains, we have heard of your virtue, Tang Sung. And you are certainly handsome. I would prefer to keep you as my husband although eating just one mouthful of your flesh would grant me immortality. You can enjoy the riches that fill this cavern. My maids will serve you. The surrounding countryside will declare you emperor. You will no longer need to serve the Tang Emperor. Instead, with my help, you will become so powerful that he will call you his older brother."

Master put his fingers in his ears. He could feel the evil in the cavern. The female monster tried to force Master to drink wine mixed with blood and to eat human flesh. This was too much. Monkey couldn't keep still anymore. But when he reverted to his true form, the monster produced a dense black cloud that hid Master. He then grabbed an iron pitchfork and began to fight. Spewing a jet of fire from her mouth, she took on the form of a being with a hundred heads, two hundred arms, and two hundred iron pitchforks. She managed to hit Monkey on the head once. A great pain shot through him, even worse than the pain from Master's skull-busting spell. He couldn't see. He couldn't hear. All he could do was moan. It took both Pigsy and Sandy to carry him away. Victorious, but angry, the monster returned to the cavern and ordered Master tied hand and foot, and tossed into the corner.

After a night of pain, Monkey recovered enough to return to the cavern, again in the form of a bee. He found Master, still tied up in a corner and whispered in his ear, "Don't lose heart. We'll save you."

This time, Pigsy led the attack, but the monster hit him in the face with her pitchfork. Howling in pain, Pigsy fled. Sandy tried next and was hit on the chest. The pain almost paralyzed him. Monkey, Pigsy, and Sandy were so weakened that they didn't know what to do. Monkey remembered the Pearls of Deliverance given him by Kwan Yin, which he had hidden on his body as hairs. He took one and blew on it. Immediately, Kwan Yin's young disciple arrived with a bamboo cage. The disciple whispered:

"This female monster is really a transcendent scorpion who once lived in the Temple of Thunder. Instead of becoming purer in Buddha's presence, it developed a desire to descend to Earth. One day, it stung the temple guardian on the hand and escaped. Its pitchfork is its sting. This bamboo cage will capture it."

The disciple also brought some Celestial balm that cured them instantly. Protected by the balm and helped by the disciple, they killed the monster and released Master.

Chapter 28

Monkey Dismissed

Master is waylaid by bandits. Monkey accidentally kills the bandit chief and gives a disrespectful funeral oration.

On the fifth day of the fifth month, the pilgrims crossed yet another range of mountains and came to a wide plain. The land looked so rich and peaceful that Master went on ahead of his disciples. But as soon as he was out of sight, robbers barred his route, shouting "Your money or your life!" Master had no money with him. He begged them to wait for his disciples who, he said, had silver. The robbers tied Master up and hung him like a basket from a nearby tree.

Now, Monkey, with his supernaturally keen hearing, had heard the whole exchange. He had Pigsy and Sandy stay behind with the baggage while he went to help Master. If the robbers were monsters, he would have happily pounded them with his iron staff until they were all beaten to mush. But these robbers were human. He knew how tenderhearted Master was and how irritated he would be if Monkey killed the humans outright. No, he did not need another skull-busting headache lesson on the need to be more compassionate and less bloodthirsty. So he took the form of a young monk—almost a boy—who carried a large number of packets wrapped in cotton.

Calling out, "Master, Master, where are you?" he was quickly seized by the robbers, who showed him his bound and gagged Master. Claiming the packets were full of gold and silver, Monkey promised to stay behind with the robbers, if they would let his Master go. The robbers released Master, who dashed away back down the road.

Monkey King chases a robber.

When the robbers opened the packets, they were furious to find them empty. The robber chief pulled his sword and began to hack away at what he thought was a boy. Monkey, resuming his normal form, decided that the robber's willingness to murder an "innocent" was enough to justify a quick tap (just one) with the iron staff. The tap, of course, killed the robber chief. Seeing this, all the other robbers got on their knees, begged forgiveness, and promised to lead lives of virtue. Master, who had watched all this from a distance, hoping for a peaceful resolution, rejoined them to weep a few tears at the killing and conduct a funeral service.

Master was irritated at Monkey for killing the robber chief. In his funeral oration, he blamed Brother Monkey for unseemly haste in the killing. This made Monkey mad, as he had only been helping Master. Why, the killing was practically an accident! Humans always surprised Monkey by their fragility.

So, he in turn gave a funeral oration.

"I only acted after the robber proved he was evil through and through by attempting to cut a 'boy' to pieces. After all my efforts on Master's behalf, I expected a little more gratitude and a little less moralizing. As the Great Saint Equal of Heaven, I have had plenty of contact with Saints and don't need to constantly listen to sermons. Plus, I only intended to knock the man out. It was not my fault that the cursed brigand had an eggshell-thin skull."

Though a holy monk, Master was also human and, in his heart, resented Monkey's tone and attitude. But he said nothing and they continued on their voyage.

Another ten li down the road, they came to an isolated farmhouse. Once Master had assured the farmer that the disciples were harmless, the farmer invited them to enter. As the farmhouse was very small, the old man put them up in the barn. The old man and his wife were decent, hard-working people, and devoted to their grandson. But their son Yang Lu had joined a band of brigands, the very one that had attacked Master. While the travelers were sleeping, Yang Lu and the robber band came to the farmhouse. They had changed their minds about reforming. When they recognized Master's horse, they rejoiced at a chance to avenge their chief. But the old man heard them plotting. He sneaked into the barn and warned the travelers to flee.

When the robbers noticed that Master and his disciples were gone, they set out after them. This time, Master made his orders to Monkey, Pigsy, and Sandy very clear. Absolutely no killing. However, attempting to fight off the robbers, Monkey accidentally decapitated Yang. Master was furious. On the spot, he wrote a document expelling Monkey from his service. Monkey, though he had a temper, was not hard-hearted. He was really sorry for the accident and begged to be forgiven. But Master was still irritated at Monkey's funeral oration, and he hardened his heart and refused to listen. Having no choice, Monkey left.

Monkey went straight to Kwan Yin and asked her to intercede. Kwan Yin was sympathetic. At the same time, she recognized that he could be violent and hasty.

"Be patient," she said. "Master will soon need you again. Rest and chat with me while I tend my garden."

Meanwhile, Master sent Pigsy ahead to scout and to beg their evening meal. After an hour, Master was worried and sent Sandy after him. Now alone, Master decided to meditate. Suddenly he saw Monkey returning with a gourd full of water.

"He is just trying to bribe his way back into the group," Master thought. "Go away," he yelled.

But Monkey hit him, knocked him out and stole his baggage. When Pigsy and Sandy returned, they found a very unhappy Master with a big, painful lump on his head. Pigsy was convinced that Monkey had decided to turn to evil, and railed against all of Monkey's bad habits.

Sandy, though, said, "There must have been some mistake. It is not in Monkey's nature to raise his hand against Master, no matter how hurt his feelings were. I will look for Monkey and get an explanation."

Leaping into the clouds, he came to Monkey's Kingdom on the Mountain of Flowers and Fruits. At the Cavern of Water, he was seized and beaten. He was stunned to see Monkey giving the orders for the beating. With some effort, he broke his bonds and flew to Kwan Yin's palace. To his amazement, there was Monkey, talking calmly to Kwan Yin. With a shout of rage, he attacked Monkey. But Kwan Yin fixed him in place with a spell and asked him to explain himself. So Sandy explained. Kwan Yin then replied,

"This can't be true. Monkey King has been here with me the entire time. He can't fool me with substitution tricks. You must return with him to the cavern and discover the truth."

In fact, Monkey King's place in the kingdom had been taken by an impostor. The fake Monkey King even planned to obtain the Holy Scriptures himself. He had a false Master, a false Pigsy, and a false Sandy. He even had a false horse. Monkey King and Sandy arrived at the cavern just in time to see his "departure."

Monkey King wasted no time. He challenged the impostor to duel, while Sandy challenged the false Sandy. They fought in front of the cavern, and fought across the sky, all the way to Kwan Yin's home. She couldn't tell them apart. When she recited the skull-busting spell for Monkey's gold circlet, they both suffered the same horrible headache. When she lifted the spell, the headache ended for both. Even the Celestial Mirror that unmasks monsters could not tell them apart. As Monkey King had long ago erased all trace of himself in the Shadowlands, the Underworld could not help.

Master could not tell them apart either, but at least realized that it was a false Monkey who had attacked him and stolen the baggage. Only Buddha could tell one from the other.

Sure he wouldn't be found out, the false monkey leapt off with the real Monkey to consult Buddha. After thousands and thousands of sky-vaults, they finally reached the Lotus throne. Buddha explained:

"Stone Monkey was not the only supernatural rebel monkey. There are three others—Horse Monkey, Monkey That Understands the Smallest Things, and Monkey of Six Ears. That one can transform himself into any being and hear anything within a thousand li. The Six-Eared Monkey is the only one who could have learned enough about Master and his disciples to attempt such a complicated impersonation."

Buddha waved his hand. The impostor monkey was transformed back into his own monkey shape. (Anyone could see the difference.) But he continued to attack, instead of begging forgiveness. Monkey King had to chase him for a thousand li before defeating and killing him. Meanwhile, Sandy and Pigsy killed the false Sandy and the false Pigsy.

They returned to Master who gladly restored Monkey as his chief disciple. (By now, Master was ashamed of having given in to his own less-kind instincts).

CHAPTER 29

Princess Steel Fan

The Mountain of Fire bars their route. Monkey tricks the Steel Fan Princess into swallowing him, but she tricks him by giving him a false fan.

Again, it was autumn, and hot. Each day became hotter than the last. The air shimmered with a heat haze. Pigsy (who was the heaviest) suffered the most but even Master, Monkey, and Sandy felt like wilted cabbages. The Horse could barely plod forward.

"I can't understand it," said Pigsy. "Here we are, high in the mountains, where usually there's even snow, but we are melting with the heat."

A passing peddler told them that the heat came from the Mountain of Fire, sixteen li to the south. A powerful Immortal, the Princess of the Steel Fan, owned a magic fan of steel, which was shaped like a banana leaf. One wave of the fan puts out the fire, a second brings wind, and a third brings rain. Without her occasional use of the fan, there would be no life at all near the mountain. She lived in the Banana Tree Cavern on Blue Cloud Mountain, about a hundred li to the east. She was the wife of Neuw Mo Wang, the Phantom King of the Buffaloes. Monkey had defeated her son Red Child earlier in their journey. Kwan Yin had taken Red Child for "reeducation." Monkey knew that the princess and her husband might not be too well disposed toward him. In fact, when he presented himself at their cavern gate and humbly asked to borrow the fan, the princess shrieked in fury, calling him "evil Monkey," "kidnapper of children," and so on.

Monkey tried to reason with her.

"Your son is now doing his "reeducation" and improving his karma by serving Kwan Yin. I only fought him in self-defense and to save my Master. I will even bring Red Child to you if you will lend me the Steel Fan."

She came rushing out of the cavern, armed with sword, ax, and machete and slashed so hard at him that she destroyed all her weapons. When she realized how powerful he was, she pulled out her steel fan and waved it at him. This blew him all the way to the palace of the Ling Ki Buddha in the Celestial Realm, at least twenty-four thousand li away. The Ling Ki Buddha welcomed Monkey and gave him a magic Fixer-of-Wind pill. With that in his mouth, Monkey could resist the fan's power.

He returned to the cavern, and they fought again. She used the Steel Fan again, but was so terrified when he didn't budge that she ran back into her cavern and sealed it shut. But Monkey had already sneaked into the cavern, as a mouse. He hid himself until he saw her servants prepare her daily jasmine tea. Quickly he turned himself into a jasmine flower. As she sipped her tea, he leaped into her mouth and she swallowed him.

Now, he called to her again from inside her belly:

"It is I, Monkey King, Great Saint Equal of Heaven. Be reasonable and lend us the Steel Fan or I will use your innards as a trapeze.

He jumped a few times, giving her such pain that she had no choice but to lend him the fan.

So Monkey returned in triumph with the fan. They continued with easy minds and no longer in despair about Flame Mountain. When they got to the mountain, Monkey waved the fan once. But the flames roared even higher. What? He had been duped by a false Steel Fan.

He called the local guardian spirit, who blamed it all on Monkey. If you recall, Monkey had once eaten all of Lao Tze's cinnabar pills to cure his hangover. When Monkey was recaptured, Lao Tze tried to retrieve the pills by melting Monkey in his Oven of Trigrams. But Monkey escaped. When he leaped out of the oven, he overturned the furnace. One of its charcoal briquettes fell to earth and became Flame Mountain. The guardian spirit suggested:

"When the Phantom King of the Buffaloes and the Steel Fan

Princess lived together, they were truly invulnerable—united in their powers. But two years ago, after Red Child was lost to them, the Phantom King left his wife for the Fox Phantom's daughter, Princess Jade Fox. Now he and Jade Fox live at the Mountain of Thunder. Perhaps you can convince him to help you get the fan from the Steel Fan Princess since she still cares for him."

Monkey King came to the Cavern of Thunder and politely asked Princess Jade Fox if she would present him to her husband so that he could petition to borrow the Steel Fan. Princess Jade Fox, however, was filled with jealousy at the thought that her husband Neuw Mo Wang might have contact with his first wife, the Steel Fan Princess. She accused Monkey of working for the Steel Fan Princess and of helping her to lure her husband back. Furious, she grabbed a spear and tried to run it through his gizzard. This broke the spear. When Monkey threatened her with his staff, she ran inside screaming in terror, and begged her husband to save her from this horrible, ugly, red-eyed monkey-monster.

When the Phantom King of the Buffaloes came out, Monkey politely made his apologies for accidentally scaring Princess Jade Fox. He again explained that Red Child was doing so well that Monkey had probably done him a favor by defeating him. Now, the Buffalo King had already received a letter from Princess Steel Fan. It alerted him to Monkey's arrival and told him that despite suffering the worst stomachache of her life, she had tricked Monkey. So, the Buffalo King responded, angrily,

"Vile red-eyed ball of monkey fur! My answer is NO, NO, NO! I know what you did to my first wife. You've insulted both my wives."

He then grabbed a giant mace and hit Monkey's head so hard he almost dislocated his shoulder. But Monkey just shook his head and moved out of range. Monkey didn't want to kill the Phantom King of the Buffaloes. After all, he had once been a friend and ally, and had even helped him against Heaven's troops. He was the one who suggested that Monkey King name himself the Great Saint Equal of Heaven. Unable to beat Monkey, Buffalo King returned to his cavern and fortified it. But it was boring to wait and wait for Monkey's next attack. When an invitation arrived for a once-a-century feast, hosted by the dragon who ruled the Pond of Sapphire, he and Princess Jade Fox were delighted. Off they went.

This gave Monkey the perfect opportunity to take the shape of the Phantom King of Buffaloes and to visit the palace of the Steel Fan Princess. She was overjoyed to see what she thought was her husband returning to her, and to hear him say:

"Dear One, I took the Princess Jade Fox as a secondary wife only because I needed her father's political support. I'm really sorry that you took that to heart. I have been so busy I haven't had time to visit you. But when I heard of how you were attacked by that lousy, red-eyed monkey (and to think we used to help him), I had to come to see if you were recovered."

Monkey then pretended to worry about the safety of the fan:

"That Monkey has a thousand schemes. Are you sure it's safe? Show me where you've been hiding it."

She took the fan out of her belt pouch. It was the size of a toothpick, but she reminded him of the spell to restore it to its true size. Grabbing the fan, the false Buffalo King immediately fled. This one was clearly the real fan. It shed a brilliant light. But Monkey didn't know how to make it smaller, and had to lug the full-sized fan.

The princess, realizing she had been tricked, sent messengers to the Pond of Sapphire. Apologizing profusely, they interrupted the Buffalo King's feast:

"Our Mistress, the Steel Fan Princess asked us to say these words to you on her behalf:

'Alas, Dear Husband, taking advantage of my continued desire for your company, Monkey King took your form and fooled me into handing over the Steel Fan. Without it we are powerless. I need your help to get it back. You are responsible for this. If you had not left me for that worthless Princess Jade Fox, he would never have succeeded.'"

The Phantom King of the Buffaloes decided he too could play at the impersonation game. Taking the form of Pigsy, he met Monkey on the route back to camp. Monkey was flattered to hear Pigsy praising Monkey to the skies for his cleverness, rather than grumbling at Monkey's overbearing ways, as he usually did.

"Elder Brother Monkey, you are truly a master strategist," said the false Pigsy. "I am sorry I couldn't see their faces when they realized that you had the Steel Fan. I feel guilty for missing all the fighting. This Steel Fan must be awkward to carry. It is as big as a large banana leaf. Allow me to unburden you."

So Monkey handed over the fan. Of course, Pigsy and the Steel Fan vanished. Monkey yelled for the real Pigsy to help him, and both rushed to fight the Buffalo King. But by then, the Phantom King of the Buffaloes, Princess Steel Fan, and Princess Jade Fox had assembled their entire army. Every time Pigsy and Monkey got close, they blew them both away with a wave of the fan. They tried to storm the cavern a dozen times and were blown away a dozen times. It looked hopeless. Even, so, they were able to kill Princess Jade Fox and destroy most of her army.

Once again, Monkey returned to the Celestial Realm to obtain Fixer-of Wind-pills from the Ling Ki Buddha for himself and Pigsy. He also asked the Buddha to send his soldiers to help. The pills were very effective. Phantom King of the Buffaloes tried to blow them away, but to his amazement they remained standing. So he changed himself to a falcon and tried to fly away, but Monkey changed to an eagle and chased him. When the falcon returned to land and became a deer, Monkey and Pigsy became wolves. Just as they were about to capture him, the Celestial generals threw a net over the Phantom King and trapped him in his true shape—that of an enormous buffalo. The Phantom King of the Buffaloes could only agree to help them. He promised that not only he, but his whole family and army of monsters would reform. So he was returned to the cavern in chains. When his wife saw that he was captured, she knelt and begged for mercy. They were both pardoned, provided they helped Monkey put out the fire. She instructed Monkey King to wave the fan forty times, which immediately put out all the flames. From then onwards she and her husband led pure lives. The countryside became green and fertile again. Even today, the people there burn incense to statues of Master, Pigsy, Sandy, and Monkey.

Chapter 30

Golden Light Jewel

The Golden Light Nation suffers from the theft of a Golden Light Jewel from the temple. Master sweeps the tower.

After hiking another fifty li, they came to the capital city of Golden Light Nation. Its teeming crowds seemed happy and prosperous. But Master noticed several monks, dressed in rags and yoked together like oxen. He pitied them and persuaded their guards to let them rest, eat, and drink a little. They were from the Temple of the Golden Aura. Curious, the travelers went to the temple, which despite its lovely name, was a ruin—desolate, dirty, and dreary. There, they found a group of feeble, ragged monks waiting for them. The night before, these monks had all dreamt that a holy pilgrim from the Tang Empire would arrive to deliver them from their situation. They explained their ill fortune:

"This kingdom is powerful but the people are restless. The king is no longer benevolent and his officials become more corrupt each day. It was not always like this. Once, our temple was the finest in the region. We possessed a holy jewel. It shed a golden aura that dazzled even in daylight. Under its influence, the king and his ministers were righteous and the people happy. Vassals volunteered tribute, and the land was at peace. Suddenly three years ago, the sky rained blood, and the Golden Light was extinguished. The vassal states then refused to provide tribute. The King and his ministers claimed the aura was destroyed because of our evil behavior. Many monks were tortured and killed. Others were enslaved. A few of us remain, but only because we are considered too old and feeble to bother with."

Master promised to plead their case when he went to present his credentials to the King. But first, he asked if he could sweep the thirteen-story main tower. He had vowed to sweep the thresholds, light incense and pray at each temple along his route. Master swept the lowest ten stories but became so tired he fell asleep. Monkey heard voices coming from the hall on the Thirteenth Floor. Changing to a mouse, he crept up, to see two fish monsters eating and drinking. He resumed his normal shape, captured them, and brought them to Master for questioning. The two begged:

"Oh, ferocious monks, don't hurt us. We are the servants of the Dragon King of Ten Thousand Virtues. He sent us here to keep an eye out for the arrival of The Great Saint Equal of Heaven. Our Dragon King of a Thousand Virtues and his son-in-law (the Nine-Headed Knight) were the ones who diverted attention with a rain of blood while they flew in and stole the Golden Light Jewel. They are afraid you will punish them when you arrive."

Of course, Master ordered his disciples to recover the Jewel. The captured monsters were sealed in an iron cage. Pigsy and Sandy took them into town.

The next morning, Master and Monkey went to present their credentials. The King welcomed them:

"Welcome to my kingdom. Your fame has come before you. The Tang Emperor is known even in these far regions as a great and virtuous monarch. I am most impressed by your credentials, but am amazed at the appearance of your disciple. He looks just like a ferocious red-eyed monkey. You, sir, look like the handsomest and kindest of holy men. I am sad that we have no truly holy monks to welcome you. It was the sins of our monks that resulted in the loss of the Golden Light Jewel from their temple tower. Since then the kingdom has been restless and the vassal states have been disobedient. In fact, war could break out at any time."

Monkey spoke for Master.

"Don't judge by appearances. A handsome face can conceal an evil heart. Your monks are innocent. We have just captured two fish monsters in the temple tower and they have revealed that the real thief is the Dragon of Ten Thousand Virtues."

Pigsy and Sandy then entered with the caged monsters. Monkey carved his name on the noses of the fish monsters. He sent them back to the Dragon King with an ultimatum—return the stolen objects or fight. When he heard the message, the Dragon King felt his liver turn to water. He would have obeyed, but his son-in-law, who was made of sterner stuff, made fun of Monkey's abilities and offered to meet him in single combat. So the son-in-law, in the shape of a nine-headed, eighteen-eyed giant, fought Monkey in front of the palace. Pigsy joined the fight but was captured after dropping his steel rake. Monkey then pretended to run away, but he sneaked into the Dragon King's underwater palace in the shape of a crab monster soldier.

Pigsy was chained to a pillar. As soon as Monkey freed him, he summoned his rake and began to destroy everything within reach. As Monkey was not a really great underwater fighter, he asked Pigsy to lure the Dragon King onto land. Pretending to weaken, Pigsy fled, chased by the Dragon King, his son-in-law, and his army. As soon as they surfaced, Monkey ambushed them from the clouds. He fractured the Dragon King's skull with his iron staff and killed him. But Monkey and Pigsy still had not located the jewel.

The next day, the Nine-Headed Knight, now the new Dragon King, attacked again with fresh soldiers. But with Monkey, Pigsy, and Sandy each engaging three of the heads and six of the arms, he had no chance, and was killed. After that, it was easy for Monkey to take his shape and trick the Princess, wife of the Nine-Headed Knight, daughter of the Dragon King, into giving him custody of the Golden Light Jewel. Then he revealed himself. She cried on learning of the death of both husband and father, but admitted that it was the theft that brought about their deaths. She vowed to atone for their sins. She would keep watch over the jewel in the temple and spend her time praying for their souls. The monks were so delighted at the return of the Jewel that they renamed the tower, the "Tower of Submission of Dragons."

CHAPTER 31

Yellow-Eyed Monster

Monkey, Pigsy, and Sandy are trapped under a Golden Bell. With the help of the Celestial Constellations and the Dragon King of the Northern Seas, they escape. The Yellow-Eyed Monster captures Master, Pigsy, and Sandy.

Each day the mountains became higher and the climbs more perilous. They eventually came to one so high and cloud-covered that no one in living memory had ever seen the peak. Following a winding path upward, they were soon above the clouds. Finally, they reached the summit. There stood an enormous temple with a bell tower that seemed to reach into the Celestial Realm.

"This must be the Temple of the Sound of Thunder, Buddha's abode. Look, even the door post is carved with the words 'Temple of the Sound of Thunder'." said Master. Monkey King had been to the real temple. He knew that this one couldn't be it. But Master was in a stubborn mood and refused to listen. Monkey tried to convince him.

"This can't be the real Temple of the Sound of Thunder. I've been there. No flesh-and-blood being can set foot there. Only souls, saints, Immortals, and other Buddhas can enter. I see monster signs. There is a black, noxious vapor coming out of all the doors and windows."

But Master insisted on entering, and Monkey had no choice but to trail after him. In the main temple hallway, they saw Buddha seated on his Lotus Throne with the five hundred Lo Han (guardian spirits) at his feet. The temple was filled with Immortals, secondary Buddhas (called "pou sa" in the Tang Empire), Tao Immortals, and spirits. Master, Pigsy, and Sandy moved closer and closer to the Lotus Throne. Monkey was desperate and could hold back no longer. Brandishing his iron staff, he sprang to attack. He didn't have a chance. Just as he raised his arm, an enormous golden bell fell from the tower. Monkey, Pigsy, and Sandy were trapped. The false Buddhas, reverting to their true forms, captured Master.

As strong as the three disciples were, they couldn't move the bell. Despite all his powers, Monkey could not escape. He made himself as large as a mountain and the bell just expanded with him. He made himself smaller than a grain of rice and the bell changed along with him. He called on all the local guardian spirits, but none could find an opening. In despair, they flew up to the Celestial Emperor to ask for help. The twenty-eight Stellar Beings arrived to attack the bell with all the tools and drills that they could find, but with no effect. Finally, the Dragon King of the Northern Seas, who had the largest horns of all the dragons, was able to make a minuscule hole in the edge of the bell. It was big enough for Monkey, after minimizing himself, to crawl out. The small hole made the bell weaker, too. Monkey King was able to shatter it with his staff and free Pigsy and Sandy. Knowing they were greatly outnumbered by the monsters, and fearing that Master would be killed if there was a full war, Monkey, Pigsy, and Sandy fled to fight another day.

This monster had named himself the Yellow-Eyed Buddha. Furious at the destruction of his golden bell, he thundered a challenge into the Heavens. If Monkey did not accept, he threatened to eat Master raw and whole, then and there. With this, Monkey, Pigsy, Sandy, and the Twenty-Eight Constellations came down to fight. After an all-day battle, the monster, whose troops were weakening, tossed a white cotton sack into the air. The sack immediately enclosed Monkey, Pigsy, Sandy, and the Constellations. The monster tied it shut and tossed it into a corner. But in his hurry, he neglected to double-knot the cord. Monkey slipped out after he made himself very small and very thin. Once out, he broke the cord and released the others.

Moving silently, they found Master inside a silver cage, meditating on his woes. Monkey easily pried the bars of the cage open and released him. He asked Pigsy and Sandy to take Master to a safe place, while he returned to the monster's false Temple of Thunder to retrieve their baggage. As everyone in the temple was deeply asleep, he had no problems sneaking into the strong room where all the loot was kept. While looking for the baggage, he saw an odd- looking silk sack. Curious, he touched it, but the minute he did, the sack made a tremendous noise that woke all the monsters. Yellow Eyes caught up, with Monkey and they fought again. Again, Yellow Eyes reached for a sack. But Monkey was onto that trick and leaped so high into the clouds that he was even above the Celestial Realm. Unfortunately, Yellow Eyes found and trapped Master, Pigsy, and Sandy in the sack instead.

Monkey King had no choice but to ask the Celestial Emperor for help once more. The Emperor sent his finest troops. But the Magical All-Encompassing Sack captured every one. Only Monkey escaped. He was becoming disheartened when Lao Tze suggested that he seek the Buddha-in-Charge-of-All-Creatures. This Buddha sent his crown prince and four field marshals to help Monkey, but after three days and nights of fighting, they, too, were captured by the Magical All-Encompassing Sack. Monkey was ready to cry with frustration and despair. Heading back for more help he met the Laughing Buddha, Mi To Fo. Mi To Fo chuckled:

"Don't worry, I came as soon as I realized that one of my young temple servants, the one who beats the drums in processions, had left without permission. He took with him the cotton bag in which the drums were stored as well as the drumsticks. I will draw a magic symbol on the palm of your hand. Transform yourself into a ripe peach. He won't be able to resist eating you. Then we'll nab him. "

Full of hope, Monkey King felt his energy return. After all, he had had a lot of experience with peaches. Off he went to the temple in the form of a gardener, so humble he was ignored by everyone, including the monster. Once in the garden, he transformed himself into the most luscious peach on the best-looking peach tree. It wasn't long before the monster, hungry from his battles, wandered by in search of a snack. That huge, luscious peach looked perfect. He swallowed it whole. He couldn't believe the pain. The "peach" seemed to be doing gymnastic vaults in his stomach. He didn't even have the strength to scream. All he could do was whisper, "Oh, Master Mi To Fo, help me! I'm so sorry that I stole the sack and the drumsticks. I promise I'll never do evil again."

With that, Mi To Fo descended from the clouds, took the sack back, and released all the prisoners. Monkey came out from Yellow Eye's insides. The "Yellow-Eyed Buddha" turned out to be just little boy with golden eyes. Mi To Fo repaired the bell. Monkey thanked all the celestial troops for their help and the travelers resumed their pilgrimage.

CHAPTER 32

The Mountain of Seven Rarities

The Mountain of Seven Rarities is carpeted with rotten fruit. The Red Python Monster attacks. They chase it to the mountain, where it swallows Monkey. Monkey puts on a show for Pigsy and Sandy. Pigsy uses his appetite to help them cross the mountain.

Several months passed in unending travel. They never spent two nights in the same place. In the spring, they came to the Village of Seven Rarities, home to five hundred families. A devout old man named Li hosted them. He warned:

"This is a beautiful area, but we have never been able to cross the Mountain of the Seven Rarities. Medlar trees, famous for their delicious pear-like fruit, grow there. The mountain is named for the seven rare qualities of these trees. One, they produce fruits that confer longevity. Two, they offer dense shade; three, no birds dare nest in their branches; four, they produce lovely rose-scented leaves. Five, the wood of even old trees has no worms; six, the leaves remain green after they fall. Finally, the fruits, though delicious when first picked, rot very quickly. When they fall, they form a viscous, slippery mass that smells so horrible that people can't bear to be closer than ten li to the mountain. These trees have taken over the mountain and the carpet of rotten fruits makes about one hundred li totally impassable."

This was disheartening news. It was stupid to be stopped by rotten

Monkey King attacks the python monster.

fruit, after having overcome so many obstacles. The old man went on:

"If that wasn't bad enough, we are threatened by a monster. It arrived here a year ago in the form of a terrible storm. It comes every night and takes all the food and crops. It ate all our livestock and killed several farmers. We hired a monk to exorcise it, but it ate the monk. It also ate the two magicians and three Tao doctors that we hired. We would be eternally grateful to if you could expel it."

Master agreed to have his disciples help. After all, they had been doing nothing else for months, years even. While Master rested in Old Man Li's home, Monkey, Pigsy, and Sandy hid in the yard and waited for the monster to appear. At midnight, such a terrible wind arose that Pigsy could not move. Sandy couldn't even open his eyes. Monkey could see, but all he could see was the light from the monster's eyes. He challenged the monster to combat. It was hard to close in, though. This monster moved so fast, it seemed to be in two places at once. At dawn the monster fled to the Mountain of Seven Rarities. Monkey, Pigsy, and Sandy followed, although the smell was so horrible that they had to hold their noses and breathe through their mouths. But they continued the chase until the exhausted monster reverted back to its true shape, that of an immense, red-scaled python. It quickly hid almost its entire length in a deep hole.

Monkey transformed his iron staff into an enormous club, and beat the part of the python that wasn't in the hole. The monster python, changing into a small winged snake, flew to a waterfall, with Monkey in hot pursuit. In a flash it took the form of a huge snake that, with one gulp, swallowed Monkey whole. Pigsy and Sandy were horrified. The Monkey-shaped lump in the snake wasn't moving. All was silent. Was this the end of the powerful monkey? All seemed lost. As they turned to bring the sad news to Master, they heard Monkey's voice from inside the python:

"Pigsy, Sandy, I heard you blubbering. It's nice to know that you would have missed me, but don't worry. I've decided that I need a bit of rest from all this fighting. Instead, I'll put on a show for you. Look."

He made his staff into a long, long, stiff rod. The python took the shape of a long, long rod. Then he made his staff into the shape of a boat and the python became boat-shaped. He even stood the monster on end and made it look like a tree. Pigsy and Sandy were impressed. But this was not very healthy for the monster, which promptly died from the stress of so many internal changes. Monkey then burst out of the corpse. They skinned it so that the villagers could have the red python skin. From then on, the village was known as the Python Skin Village.

But they still had to somehow cross one hundred li of rotten, stinking, slippery, and viscous medlar. Fortunately, while Monkey had been fighting, Pigsy had gotten so hungry that he ate one of rotten fruits. Despite the horrible odor, the fruit was really tasty. It had been quite a while since Pigsy felt he had eaten as much he needed. Taking his favorite form, that of a mountain-sized pig, he opened his enormous snout and just scooped up the fruit. Once again, Pigsy had proved that his talents were of special value to the expedition.

Chapter 33

Saving a King and His Princess

Monkey helps cure the king's illness, caused by the abduction of his wife. The princess is protected by a tunic of needles. The monster has three rattles that produce smoke, fire, and sand. Monkey and the princess obtain the rattles by trickery.

In summer they came to the Nation of Purple Mountains. This was a civilized nation, organized much like the Tang Empire. They had to register with the officials when they entered the capital city, and convince the immigration officials that they represented the Tang Emperor, and proclaim that their mission was a holy one. In the morning, after they had settled their baggage at an inn, Master called on the king and explained his mission. The king, a thin, pale man, was kindly looking, but seemed sad. He was obviously extremely ill.

In the evening, Monkey and Pigsy went to the market to buy rice and vegetables. Hearing shouting and crying, they followed the sounds to huge crowd gathered around a proclamation posted on a wall. It called upon all the kingdom's doctors to come to the palace and heal the King of his mortal illness. Monkey brought a copy of the proclamation back to Master.

"Could you help?" wondered Master.

Master and Monkey offered their help at the palace, but there was one problem. Monkey was so strange-looking that the court mandarins were afraid that the king would be frightened to death from just one look at him. They allowed Monkey to take the king's pulse, but only from a distance. They laid a silk thread across the king's wrist, but hid the rest of the king behind the brocade curtains of a canopy bed.

Monkey's senses were so acute that, touching only the silk thread, he was still able to diagnose the king's ailment. This, the Malady of Separation, was based on some terrible emotional loss due to separation from a loved one. Monkey could restore the body to health, but the disease would return unless the cause was removed. Using his special skills, Monkey gathered a hundred ingredients. Begging a cup of wine from the Dragon King's palace, he made an elixir. As soon as the king drank the elixir his physical health returned. But he looked as sad as ever, and still complained of an ache in his heart. Monkey then asked him to explain the true origin of his illness.

Sighing, the king said:

"Very few kings can choose whom to marry. I was fortunate. My queen, Princess Gold, was also my true love. We lived happily and harmoniously for many years. Three years ago, a monster appeared in the palace garden. It kidnapped my queen and her handmaidens. Each full moon it returns to kidnap more of my subjects and to take jewels from the palace treasury. I have thought of nothing else since. I can't eat. I can't sleep. And tonight the moon is once again full."

Of course, Monkey, Pigsy and Sandy prepared to ambush the monster. Master and the king retired, for safety, to the inner palace. The king gave Monkey a carved jade ring. If he found the queen, Monkey could show it to her as proof the king had sent him.

This monster, who called himself General Strong Arm, appeared just as the full moon rose in the sky. Instead of encountering the usual horde of screaming humans, he found himself facing a monkey, a pig, and a beetle-browed monk. His lance broke in the first face-off, but he wouldn't yield. He took three rattles from his belt and shook them. A storm of fire, smoke, and sand filled the sky, allowing him to run back to his lair.

Monkey took up the chase and searched the surrounding countryside. When he saw a distant fire-peaked mountain surrounded by a huge black cloud of smoke and sand, he knew it had to be the monster's lair. He decided against just charging right to the gates and challenging the monster to a duel. To use his brains would take a lot less effort. Changing himself into a wise-looking Tao doctor, complete with long white beard, he knocked at the gate of the monster's cavern. Announcing himself as a "Doctor" of Tao miracles, he offered to solve any problems for a fee. Monster General Strong Arm personally invited him in, explaining:

"What good fortune you appeared. I have a beautiful wife, Princess Gold, who still misses her former husband. She won't let me near her. Now, it would normally not be a problem since I am much stronger than she is. But she wears a magic Tunic of Needles that was given her by an Immortal. If she doesn't want to be touched, all the needles stick out and she becomes a human porcupine. I'm covered with wounds from attempting to touch her."

The "Tao doctor" offered to mix a special elixir. It would make her happy to be his wife and she would take off the Tunic of Needles. But, he said, he had to be alone with her. So Monster General Strong Arm allowed the false Tao doctor into the women's quarters in the palace. The queen was wearing her needle-covered tunic. Keeping a safe distance, Monkey, the false doctor, quickly showed her the jade and gold ring. As she kissed the ring, she sobbed with relief:

"Dear Tao doctor, you give me hope again. I was afraid I would die here. This monster is very powerful. He possesses three rattles, attached to his belt. When shaken, one produces a storm of fire, another, smoke, and the third, sand."

Monkey answered:

"I am a better fighter, but as soon as I am close to winning, the monster will shake his rattles and escape. I told him that I could make you become a loving wife. If you can pretend to be interested in him, we should be able to get the magic rattles."

They made a plan. Monkey, still as the false Tao doctor, announced he had successfully transformed the princess. While General Strong Arm put on his finest garments so he could impress her, Monkey returned to her room and transformed himself into a sandalwood box. Moments later, the monster ran in:

"Beautiful Princess Gold! Is it true? Are you willing to stop being so prickly and to allow me to embrace you?"

Pretending to be sweet and docile, she whispered:

"Dear husband, life is too short to waste in useless regret. I've actually forgotten what my former husband looked like. But you've treated me more like a prisoner than a wife. You don't let my handmaids near me. You don't trust me at all. I'll take off my tunic of needles if you show me you trust me. Put your three rattles in this treasure box. I have no wish to hug a man with three loud, bulging rattles around his waist."

The monster thought about this, but couldn't see a catch. He tossed the belt and rattles in the box. Monkey was so pleased with his trick, though, that he laughed. When the monster saw the box shaking with laughter, he let out a roar and attacked it. In the fight, Monkey lost his grip on the rattles. It seemed better to flee, and try again. Fortunately, Princess Gold was good at acting. She seemed so horrified that a "demon" had tried to steal the rattles, that the monster had no idea she was involved.

Monkey slipped back into Princess Gold's quarters in the form of a fly and settled on her ear. He whispered his plan. He would take the form of her maid, Precious Flower. The princess would invite the monster to an intimate supper in her quarters. You can be sure the monster was delighted. The princess served the finest of salty and spicy foods. These made him terribly thirsty, so he drank gallon after gallon of wine. Of course, he became quite drunk and even more foolish than a drunken human.

While all this was going on, Monkey transformed a dozen of his hairs into fleas and set them to bite General Strong Arm. Soon, he itched so badly that he took off his jacket and asked the princess to use a steel backscratcher on him. While she was scratching him, she said:

"Dear husband, you have so many bites that you are bleeding. We have to really get rid of the source of the fleas. It's clear that they're coming from the rattles. Give them to me and I will soak them in brine. That will kill the fleas."

The monster, in agony, and with his brain dulled by the wine, agreed. Monkey, of course changed three hairs from his head into the form of the rattles, and switched them for the real ones. Still in the maid's form, he carefully wrapped the real rattles in cotton and sneaked them out of the cavern. Once outside, he resumed his real shape and shouted a challenge to battle. The monster grabbed his jacket, took up his rattles, and came storming out to attack Monkey.

They fought as before. When the monster began to weaken, he shook his rattles. But nothing happened. No storm of fire, no storm of smoke, and no storm of sand. He spotted the real rattles tied around Monkey's waist. All was lost. Monkey prepared to pulverize General Strong Arm with his iron staff.

But from the clouds he heard the voice of Kwan Yin:

"Don't kill him, Great Saint Equal of Heaven. This is a jackal, one of my mounts. He was only obeying my orders. I sent him to punish the king for violating a ban on hunting on temple grounds and for killing a pair of pheasants. Because the pheasants were three years old, I ordained that the king should be separated from his wife for three years to teach him more compassion for other beings and to respect the temple grounds."

Of course, Monkey put down his staff. The monster vanished. There would be no more kidnappings and terror. No longer needed, the Tunic of Needles also vanished. Princess Gold and her husband, the king, were reunited. He offered many prayers at the temple and ruled more wisely and kindly than before.

Chapter 34

Spider Monsters

In the Cavern of the Spires of Silk, seven young females capture Master, Pigsy, and Sandy with their silk. Monkey frees them only to see them poisoned by an evil Thousand-Eyed Monster.

Autumn, winter, and spring passed. Except for the usual storms, attacks by brigands, minor monsters, and such, their travels were quite uneventful. This countryside was peaceful. The harvest looked good. The travelers came to a large mansion. Since the fierce appearance of his disciples usually scared unsuspecting humans, Master usually was the one who went to doors to beg for their evening rice. Pigsy, Sandy, and Monkey would wait for him in a nearby campsite. At this house, Master saw four young ladies who were sewing and three others playing ball. They all welcomed him warmly and asked him to wait on the verandah while four of them prepared a meal. Soon they were busy mincing human flesh to make meatballs. Master smelled the meat and realized that something was very wrong. When he tried to leave, they barred his route and tied him to a post. White silk spun out from the tips of their fingers, and covered all the doors and windows. Monkey became worried when Master didn't return. While Pigsy and Sandy stayed behind to guard the baggage, he went on ahead. He spotted the farmhouse. The windows and doors seemed to be completely covered with white fibers. This looked odd. Before charging in, he needed information, so he thumped his iron staff on the ground and summoned a local guardian spirit. The spirit explained:

"Your Master must be in trouble. This mansion is actually the Cavern of Spires of Silk. It is inhabited by female monsters who live on human flesh. Also near here is the Cavern of Purification of Earth. That one is inhabited by male monsters. They are the adopted sons of the females in the Cavern of Spires of Silk. They took over the dwellings after chasing away the Immortals who were the rightful owners. Be very careful. They are powerful and dangerous."

As Monkey stood watching, the female monsters retracted the silk back into their fingertips. The mansion returned to its normal appearance. Monkey, needing to enter the house unobserved, took the form of a fly. He listened thoughtfully as the women chatted about their plans to eat the nice, juicy, tender monk later that evening. First, they went off to swim in the deep pond in their garden. They left all their clothes on the bank, and dove in. As they played, Monkey changed himself into a large eagle, snatched up their clothes in his talons, and flew off. He was a bit reluctant to kill seven females—even female monsters. And Master seemed safe for the moment.

Back at the camp, he told his companions what had happened. Pigsy complained:

"Why so tender-hearted all of a sudden? Monsters are monsters, no matter what pleasing shape they take. Well, I have no such scruples, especially when Master may become stewed monk tonight."

With that, Pigsy, went right to the gate, battered it down with his rake and entered. The young women had just dressed and were cursing the eagle that had stolen their nicest clothes. Pigsy challenged them to combat. They all screamed and fled. He didn't know which one to chase first, so he ended up wildly chasing all of them. Huffing and panting, he had to stop and catch his breath. At this point, they surrounded him and used their "silk" to wrap such a cocoon around him that he could barely breathe. These seven "girls" were actually, seven insects who had achieved transcendence. Monkey, who was a little embarrassed by Pigsy's criticism, had followed him. Seeing him captured, he gave a tremendous shout, leaped over the wall and ran to attack them. The seven women retreated into their house, again sucking the silk back into their fingers (which released Pigsy). Then they called their sons for help. Before Pigsy and Monkey could head back to their campsite, the seven sons arrived and barred their route. Pigsy bravely attacked them, but they transformed into ten thousand venomous insects and stung him so many times that his eyes swelled shut. Monkey dealt with the insects by quickly changing his hairs into a thousand birds that ate them all. Monkey, Pigsy, and Sandy ran back to the Cavern of Seven Spires.

"Release him," they shouted in unison, their angry voices rattling even the air. There was no response. All they heard was the voice of Master calling for help. The seven female monsters had fled, leaving him behind.

Not the least interested in lingering in this monster-infested territory, they moved on instead of making camp. After several hours, they came to a palatial home, with the name "Hermitage of the Yellow Flower" carved on the door post. Though it looked like a very rich, respectable, and safe house, it wasn't. In fact, the seven female monsters were hiding there. This was the house of their Honorary Uncle, a Tao doctor. After the women told him about the eagle, birds, scary pig, and monkey, he knew he could not defeat the disciples in open combat. Using his Taoist learning, he prepared twelve powerful poison pills and hid them in twelve red candies. He also prepared four black candies. These were safe. When the travelers arrived, he came out and welcomed them with kind words and a smiling face. Master, who was, after all human and had no special powers, was exhausted, hungry, and very happy at the thought of food and rest. The Tao doctor personally prepared the food to make sure it was not contaminated from meat or animal products. It was an excellent meal.

After dinner, the Tao doctor brought out the candies. Monkey noticed that the Tao doctor put red candies on their plates and black ones on his own. This made him suspicious, so he offered to exchange his tasty-looking red ones for the Tao doctor's plain black ones. But the Tao doctor acted very offended that Monkey wouldn't let him be a proper host. Reluctantly, Pigsy and Sandy each ate one. They had no sooner swallowed than they collapsed as if dead. Master, who had just touched one lightly with his fingertips, fell down in a faint. At this, Monkey overturned the table.

"You poisoned them, you no-good, evil doctor!" he screamed.

Hearing the commotion, the seven female monsters came charging out, spinning their silk and trapping Master, Pigsy, and Sandy. Monkey escaped by leaping one hundred li straight up. These women could only be spider monsters, thought Monkey. He waited until they retracted the silk. Then he attacked, transforming his hairs into monkeys armed with pitchforks. When the seven women threw out their silk, the monkeys just rolled them up in it using the pitchforks. Once captured, Monkey knocked them all out with his staff. As he watched, they resumed their true shape as spiders. The Tao doctor changed himself into a giant with a thousand eyes that shot out poisonous rays of light. When the rays hit Monkey, the fierce pain sent him digging into the earth to escape. Underground, a local guardian spirit answered his cry for help:

"You have been fighting not a Tao doctor, but a Thousand-Eyed Monster. Only Kwan Yin can help you."

Waiting until dark, Monkey transformed one of his hairs back to one of the magic pearls that Kwan Yin had given him when they began their voyage. When he blew on the pearl, his pain eased and Kwan Yin came. He must have interrupted her daily routine as she still had an embroidery needle and an embroidery basket in her hand. Side-by-side, they faced the Thousand-Eyed Monster. She tossed her embroidery needle at it. The poisonous rays from its eyes disappeared and it fell to earth in its true form, that of a large centipede. Kwan Yin gathered the centipede and the seven spiders and locked them inside her basket. She gave Monkey three antidote pills that restored Master, Pigsy, and Sandy to health.

CHAPTER 35

The Mountain of Lions and Elephants

Monkey uses his shape-changing power and persuades the monster soldiers to flee the Cavern of the Three Monster Kings. Monkey pierces the Magic Flask of Pure Yin and Yang Essence and escapes.

After resting three days, the pilgrims continued on their way. It was fall. They were feeling quite confident until they met an old hermit who said:

"Turn back, turn back. This is the Mountain of Lions and Elephants. It is the most dangerous of regions. Ferocious, flesh-eating monsters live here. They have hundreds of thousands of monster soldiers. These beings are so powerful that even Buddha's guardians, the Lo Han, pay them tribute. The Twenty-eight Constellations, the Four Dragon Kings, and the Eight Immortals of Heaven dare not leave them off of invitations to Celestial banquets."

Monkey was convinced the Old Man was simply exaggerating. After all, hadn't they already vanquished many monsters? Could these really be worse? He assured Master that it would be safe go ahead. But even Monkey became more concerned when he met the Pole Star Saint, who had come expressly to warm him about these extremely powerful monsters and to advise Monkey to be careful in his use of shape changes. There was no way to avoid the monsters when crossing the mountain.

Monkey took the form of a green fly. It was one of his favorite transformations, and very practical for spying. Buzzing about, he heard a herald monster order an assembly of monsters to kill all green flies. Immediately, Monkey took the form of a mandarin monster and tried to go forward in that shape. The "herald" blocked him because he didn't recognize the "mandarin" as a local resident. Monkey insisted that he was really a chief aide who had just been promoted and brought over from another cavern. The herald demanded to see his medallion of office. Fortunately, Monkey had seen one of the other monsters wearing such a medallion and was able to transform one of his hairs into a reasonable copy. He informed the herald that his new job was to unmask impostors. To prove they were real heralds, all heralds had to list the powers of the great monster-kings of the mountain.

As he listened to the heralds chant a list of monster-king powers, Monkey learned that the Great Monster King Giant Maw could make his mouth so large he could swallow ten thousand men in one bite. The second, Dragon-Faced King, could make himself one hundred li tall, and he killed by touching the nose of his adversary. The third, King Commander of the Wind, could raise a windstorm so strong it would level mountains. His treasure was a flask of pure yin and yang liquid. It would dissolve anyone and anything. According to the heralds, the three kings were determined to share Master's flesh and to kill Monkey King and so avenge all the monsters that Monkey had killed.

Wasting no time, Monkey announced that the heralds were "impostors." Before they could react, he killed them. Taking the shape of the chief herald, he entered the Cavern of the Three Monster Kings. Once inside, he announced to all the lowly monster soldiers and servants:

"Monkey King, Great Saint Equal of Heaven, is coming to kill you all. You should flee. Why should you stay and fight for your kings? You aren't going to share the feast of the Holy Pilgrim's flesh anyway."

The soldiers and servants, seeing the logic, fled.

Once the cavern was empty of monster soldiers, Monkey decided to have some fun. He transformed himself into a huge green fly. When the three kings returned, they were not fooled, and knew immediately the green fly was Monkey. Whacking away with the biggest fly swatters they could find, they chased after him. Monkey flew so fast that they couldn't hit him. Swat! Swat! They managed to swat each other black and blue and to break almost all the furniture in the cavern. In fact, they looked so silly that Monkey couldn't help laughing. He laughed so hard that he popped back into his own form. (It takes concentration to maintain an alien shape.) The three monsters seized their chance, jumped on him, and shoved him into the Magic Flask of Pure Yin and Yang. Inside, Monkey saw a great red flame coming to devour him. He escaped the flame, but it turned into a vile green vapor that surrounded him. Just as he began to weaken, he remembered that he still had one of Kwan Yin's magical talismans. When he took it out and blew on it, it became an extremely sharp needle, which he used to puncture a hole in the neck of the flask. The hole was, of course, really tiny, but he made himself really tiny, too, and slipped through. Very carefully, he transformed himself into a cricket and hopped out of the cavern.

He returned to the campsite and got Pigsy to join him while Sandy guarded Master. The First Monster King responded to their challenge:

"No need to tear up the countryside in futile combat. I will make just three attacks. If you survive, I promise to give up."

Monkey agreed. The monster took an enormous mallet and hit Monkey on the head. Nothing happened to Monkey, but the mallet bounced off and landed one hundred li away. Next, he took an enormous sword and cut Monkey in two.

"Oh, that tickles!" giggled Monkey, as his top and bottom half immediately rejoined.

Now, the monster transformed himself into a creature with an enormous mouth, and swallowed Monkey, the forest and most of the surrounding mountainside in one bite. Fortunately, Pigsy, who had been resting just out of range, avoided the mouth and escaped. They had all been so impressed by the stories about the power of the local monsters that Pigsy was sure it was the end of Monkey. Master, when he heard the sad news, shed many tears.

The First Monster King was certainly pleased with himself. He returned to his cavern and boasted of his success. The Second and Third Monster Kings, however, advised him to quickly vomit up Monkey because they had heard that he was not digestible. But none of the medicines worked. Monkey stayed put. He had been in these situations many times. They heard him say:

"Why should I go out into the cold night, when it's so warm and cozy in here? I will make furniture out of the bones and flesh. I could start a fire and use my staff to make a chimney in the monster's skull. What fun it will be!"

Fire? Chimney? The Monster King was in agony. He begged Monkey to leave. He even promised to help Monkey King and his companions cross the mountains. So Monkey crawled up the monster's throat. But the monster still planned to win. Just as Monkey reached his mouth, the monster king tried snap it shut and grind Monkey up with his teeth. Monkey beat a quick retreat and returned to the monster's stomach. He transformed one of his hairs into a long cord, and attached it to the monster's intestines. Using his iron staff as a brace he came out, very carefully. Of course he was attacked from all sides, but he pulled on the cord and the First Monster King screamed in unimaginable pain. The three monsters had met their match. Promising to reform, they begged Monkey to spare them.

When Monkey returned to camp, Master was so happy to see him that he fainted with joy. Pigsy wasn't half as happy. He was just beginning to enjoy being the number one disciple. So instead of greeting Monkey with a hearty welcome, he complained that Monkey had deliberately stayed away so long just to keep them worried.

The next day they set out, hoping to continue their journey without any more interference. But they walked right into an ambush by the Three Monster Kings, who had never intended to keep their promises. What a battle! While Monkey King fought the First King, Pigsy engaged the Second, and Sandy the Third King. During the fight, the Second Monster King took the form of a dragon, elongated his nose, and inhaled Pigsy. Fortunately, both Monkey King and Sandy had better luck, beating off their opponents. But Pigsy needed rescuing immediately. These monsters were indeed powerful.

That night, Monkey sneaked into the Second Monster King's cavern in the shape of a mouse and found Pigsy sitting in a big pot of water. Pigsy was yelling for help and angrily calling Monkey names for not rescuing him yet. Hearing all the name-calling, and feeling more than a little put out, Monkey decided to trick Pigsy. Changing himself into a flea, he leaped onto Pigsy's ear and whispered:

"Your time is up. I'm the emissary from the Lord of the Shadowlands, here to remind you to prepare to be judged. I might, however, change my mind, if you made it worth my while."

Having no choice, Pigsy confessed that he had some silver hidden in his other ear. He begged the "emissary" to take it and free him. Laughing, Monkey resumed his real shape and freed Pigsy. They burst into the monster's main room and attacked. When the Second Dragon Monster King tried to elongate his nose again, Monkey just elongated his staff and stuck it up the monster's nose. The monster king was carried off to Master, his long nose impaled. Now, Master could never believe that any being was truly evil. He decided to pardon the monster on condition that he persuade the First and Third Monster Kings to help the travelers on their journey.

Well, the Second Monster persuaded his allies, all right, but not to reform. After much discussion, posturing, and expressions of concerns about noses and stomachs, they decided that trickery was smarter than fighting. They would pretend to help the travelers. Master was placed in a litter, carried by monster underlings. The monster kings walked side by side with Monkey, Pigsy, and Sandy. All went well for about forty li. They were now close to the main citadel of the First Monster King, whose powers gained in strength as he neared his home. As soon as they were in view of it, the Monster Kings engaged Monkey, Pigsy, and Sandy in combat while the litter bearers flew into the citadel with Master. Master had no idea he was being kidnapped, since the curtains of the litter were drawn. In fact, the litter bearers were under orders to be gentle and move smoothly, because fright would cause Master's flesh to taste acrid.

This time, the Three Monster Kings brought out their army. Thirty thousand seasoned monster-warriors would fight against Monkey, Pigsy, and Sandy. The combat raged all night and all day. Finally, weak with fatigue, Pigsy and Sandy were captured. Even Monkey was so tired that he could not escape capture. Now, they were thrown into the same cell as Master. Was this the end?

Happy monsters spent the night celebrating in the citadel. Monkey saw them preparing an enormous cauldron to cook all four of them. While pretty monster-maids flirted with the guards, Monkey transformed one of his hairs into an image of himself, while he made himself invisible. He leaped into the sky and begged one of the sky dragons to help by going into the cauldron and preventing it from heating. So, when the cage containing Master, Pigsy, Sandy, and the hair-monkey was lowered into the cauldron, they were amazed to find the water not boiling, but warm, and just right for a bath. Monkey said a sleep spell, and all the monsters fell asleep. He hauled Master, Pigsy and Sandy out of the cauldron, and they all rushed for their campsite. Unfortunately a thunderstorm slowed their progress and woke the monsters, who charged out after them.

This time during the combat, the First Monster King captured Master again and locked him in a cage in the cavern of the Third Monster King. Then, in full view of Monkey, Master, and Pigsy, he cooked and ate a cow to which he had given the shape of Master. The disciples, fooled by the trick, were heartbroken. It had to be the end. Master had no special powers to save himself.

With great sadness, they leaped up to the sky to find Buddha and to ask him for permission to continue the journey without Master, and to take the sacred scriptures back to China. Master's death would not be in vain. Monkey also wanted his gold circle removed. To their great relief, Buddha answered:

Your Master is not dead. You were fooled. He is hidden in the Cavern of the Third King. If you can lure those monsters to the Celestial Realm, I, Buddha will subdue them.

The three disciples hastily flew to the Third Monster King's cavern. They arrived just in time, too. The monster kings' chief chefs were rolling out puff pastry, planning to create a human meat turnover, with Master as the filling. Monkey blew hard, managing to put out all the lamps in the cavern. Pigsy and Sandy, yelling and thumping, made so much noise in the dark that the monsters thought the entire Celestial army was after them. Once again, the monster soldiers all deserted. But the three kings came out fighting. They were so eager to kill Monkey, Pigsy and Sandy, that they pursued them all the way into the Celestial Realm. Suddenly, Buddha appeared and tossed three silk handkerchiefs at them. Immediately, each was tied up inside a handkerchief. Monkey opened the handkerchiefs, to find, not monster kings, but a white lion, a green elephant, and a golden eagle. Buddha tossed them out of the Celestial Realm, and all the way down to the Shadowlands where they would be judged for their sins.

Chapter 36

A Thousand Children Saved

Monkey saves a thousand children who would have been killed. He challenges the Tao Doctor to combat. Pigsy gets a great feast.

It was bitterly cold when they came to the City of Children in the Country of Deep Lakes. In the snow-covered city, amid the usual wintry market scenes and crowds, they were disturbed to see cages that were filled with children hanging from lampposts. When Master asked their innkeeper about this, he replied:

"Three years ago, a Tao doctor with a beautiful daughter came to visit the City of Children. The king fell madly in love with her, married her and made her father, the Tao doctor, his prime minister. Last year, the king fell ill. He became pale, his body ached all over, and he began to waste away. The Tao doctor said that, not only could he cure the king, he could make an elixir of immortality. He already had ninety-nine of the necessary one hundred ingredients, but needed one more. That one required the hearts and livers of one thousand children. So the king held a lottery, to choose the thousand victims. Those are the caged children."

"This great evil cannot be allowed. Even if I die, I must speak against it when I present my credentials," a horrified Master announced.

Sandy, who was the most sensible and cautious disciple, advised:

"Master, we can't do the children any good if you are beheaded. Though Monkey, Pigsy, and I have enough power to free the children by force, it can't be done without killing thousands of the king's subjects. We need information. We need to see if the Tao doctor is human. Can we change his mind? If he is a monster, then we can kill him."

That night, Monkey called together all the local guardian spirits and ordered them to stir up a great storm. Under cover of the storm, they were to take all the children out of the city and hide them. Monkey would give a signal when it was safe to return the children.

The next day, Master called on the king. Monkey, in the shape of a ladybug, was hidden in his hat. While Master was presenting his credentials and going through the elaborate greeting ceremony, Monkey observed the king, who indeed was thin and feeble. The Tao doctor, in contrast, was big and strong, with heavy muscles. He treated Master with disdain and laughed when Master tried to preach about the importance of compassion and goodness. And he scowled when Master stated that spiritual immortality could only be achieved through living many lives of perfection, not by swallowing an elixir or pills. During the speeches and greetings, Monkey's keen eyes detected that black, noxious, aura, the one encountered around monsters, fogging the air around the Tao doctor. He stayed behind—now in the form of a cricket—when Master took his leave.

Master had been gone only a few moments when the head of the palace guard ran in to tell the king and the prime minister that all the captive children were missing. The Tao doctor, not the least upset, said:

"Heaven has blessed us. We don't need the children. Tang Sung, the Holy Monk from the Tang Empire, has lived ten thousand lives of perfection. His heart and liver will be far better for my immortality elixir than the hearts and livers of even ten thousand children."

Monkey rushed back to the inn with news. Quickly, he smeared mud from the inn yard on Master's face. With one of his magic spells, he changed Master into the very image of Monkey himself. Monkey, in turn, took on the form of Master. When the king's soldiers arrived to arrest Master, Monkey, in Master's form, willingly surrendered and accompanied them back to the king, whistling a happy tune all the way. The king and Tao doctor were surprised to find "Master" not the least bit upset that his heart and liver were to be made into elixir. In fact, "Master" was eager to help. Taking a knife, he sliced open his chest.

"So, which do you want," he asked cheerfully, "the red, the yellow, or the white one?"

It was obvious this was no human. The Tao doctor attacked "Master," who by now had returned to Monkey form. Into the sky they both leaped, fighting furiously. After about ten bouts, the Tao doctor took the form of a rainbow-colored cloud and disappeared. Back at the palace, the king's wife suddenly changed into a gold and silver cloud and vanished, also. The king fainted. When he awoke, freed from spells and enchantments, he lamented his decision to sacrifice the thousand children. As he was weeping and tearing his clothes, Monkey gave the signal. The guardian spirits returned the children. Everyone in the kingdom was hysterical with joy. Perhaps they learned that there should be limits to what a king can order and to what a people should sacrifice.

Once the children were reunited with their families, Monkey was eager to get started on the search for the Monster, but Pigsy was not:

"You, my scrawny Monkey brother, may be satisfied with a few berries and nuts for dinner. But I haven't had a square meal for a month. To fight, a pig needs NOURISHMENT."

When they heard this, the people of the city joined the king and his court to make an enormous feast. Pigsy was able to eat as much as he wished. Finally, with his strength restored, he and Monkey leaped into the clouds to look for the Tao doctor.

Sixty li to the east of the capital, a guardian spirit told them that the Tao doctor lived nearby in the Cavern of Nine Willows. It wasn't hard to find. The Tao doctor and his "daughter" were lamenting their lost chance to eat the hearts and livers of all those children, or at least a liver and heart from a holy monk. After all, the magic elixir had never been meant for the king. Unable to escape the fury of Pigsy and Monkey, they had to fight. Pigsy killed the Tao doctor with an enormous blow from his rake. On death, the doctor became a white deer. Monkey's staff killed the "queen," who reverted to her white fox form. That explained the king's health problems. She was a were-fox. Were-foxes lived by sapping the life force of humans. Once she was gone, the king's health quickly returned. He had learned his lesson, and, from then on, he devoted himself to the welfare of his people.

Chapter 37

Master Is Tricked

Master overrules Monkey and they save a girl.
Master is kidnapped by a female monster who wants him as her husband. Monkey fails with one trick but succeeds with another.

It was spring. The formerly barren hillsides were alive with green. Flowers, birds, and sunshine filled the days. The pleasant route seemed safe, and they traveled cheerfully, until they came to a dense pine forest. Sunlight barely filtered beyond the tops of the trees. The ground was carpeted in pine needles, muffling the sounds of their footsteps. At the first clearing they came to, Master stopped to rest while Pigsy and Sandy foraged for edible berries and nuts. Monkey leaped into the clouds to scout the route ahead. Master was left to guard the baggage. His meditations were interrupted by screams. He ran toward the sound to find a girl tied to a tree. Her clothes were torn and bloody. She sobbed:

"Help me! My family was ambushed by bandits when we were traveling. I don't know if my parents are alive or dead. The robbers knocked me out. I woke up to find myself tied to this tree. My father is a wealthy merchant, and the robbers must have gone to their den to share out the loot. Please save me."

By this time, Monkey, Pigsy, and Sandy had returned. Master ordered Pigsy to untie the girl, but Monkey stopped him. When scouting the area, he had felt an evil presence, and a trace of monster aura. Now, he saw the dark aura surrounding the girl. Master, remembering that he had been captured the last time he ignored Monkey's advice, hardened his

Beautiful girl tries to tempt young monk—Monkey King in disguise.

heart. He agreed to leave her bound to the tree. As they walked away, her cries became ever more piercing and pitiful. Finally, Master could stand it no longer and ordered Monkey to untie her. Monkey refused, but Pigsy obeyed. So she joined the group. Because monks were forbidden contact with females, she had to walk in the middle of their group. Master and Pigsy walked six feet ahead of her, and Monkey and Sandy walked six feet behind her.

That evening, they came to an apparently deserted monastery. The entrance was overgrown with weeds. Cracks zigzagged across the pavement, and fallen roof tiles and loose bricks littered the ground. Even so, the entrance bell looked like it worked. Monkey tried it. A group of monks came out of hiding. The oldest addressed them:

"Welcome, travelers. I must apologize for hiding, but we were afraid that you were bandits or monsters. We deliberately let the front of the temple go to ruin so that evil-doers would ignore us. This is the Monastery of Contemplation, and you are invited to dine with us. You can put the young lady in the guest tower. She looks like she's been a victim of robbers. She will be safe there."

The monks offered them a good dinner of rice and vegetables. Even Pigsy was satisfied, though he would have preferred some candy and dessert, too. But the next morning, Master felt ill. He had a high fever and was very weak. While the monks nursed Master, Monkey spent a few days exploring the temple and talking to the young acolytes. He soon became aware that they seemed to be terrified of something. Under his skillful questioning, they admitted that after the travelers' arrival, one of the young monks had disappeared. The next morning, all they had found were his bones. Some of the young acolytes were sure they heard strange noises and saw strange shadows dart about their dormitory hall. There must be a monster or evil ghost haunting their temple. What could they do? Monkey suspected that the girl they had rescued had a role in this. He told all the young acolytes to camp out together in the main temple that night while he kept watch.

As soon as they had gone off to the main temple, Monkey transformed himself into a handsome young acolyte. When the moon rose, a sudden windstorm blew the dust so violently that even Monkey had to close his eyes a moment. When he opened them, he saw the girl, now dressed as splendidly as a princess. Her lovely voice murmured:

"Oh, you are so handsome. Why are you wasting your time with sutras and prayers? Come with me and we can enjoy so many pleasures."

She came nearer to kiss him. At that, Monkey reverted to his true form. A human would have screamed in terror. But the girl made two swords appear, and attacked. As they fought, she retreated toward the gate. Just as Monkey was about to reach her, she created a windstorm. The whirling sand forced Monkey to close his eyes for a second. During that second, she transformed one of her slippers into an image of herself and escaped. The false "girl" was very light and flew quickly, high into the sky. While Monkey was trying to catch up, the real girl returned in the form of a large dust devil, entered the temple, and whirled Master to her home, the Bottomless Cavern. Master had been her target all along. As he was very handsome, she decided she would force him to marry her.

Meanwhile, Monkey chased the false "girl" until he was finally close enough to hit her with his staff. Out of the sky fell a woman's slipper. Frustrated at being tricked, Monkey flew back to the Monastery to find Pigsy and Sandy frantically searching for Master. Monkey needed more information. Still frustrated, he uprooted a dozen pine trees to get the attention of the local guardian spirits. They came running, telling him that Master had been captured by the Monster Queen of the Bottomless Cavern. With the location known, Monkey, Sandy, and Pigsy dashed off.

Pigsy was the first to reach the cavern. There he saw two pretty female-monster soldiers.

"This should be easy. They barely look strong enough to hold up their spears," he said to himself. Pigsy swaggered up to their gate.

"Ho, lassies. Be good girls and announce that the Great Pig Monk has come to talk to your queen. By the way, did you know those spears spoil your good looks?"

The female-monster soldiers were furious at his bad manners. So disrespectful! Without hesitation, they used their iron spear shafts to beat him up. Then they lectured on the need for ugly pigs to learn prettier manners. Almost too sore to crawl, Pigsy returned to Monkey, covered with bruises, moaning, groaning, and cursing all deceptively pretty monster soldiers. Monkey laughed so hard that he split his pants, but finally he put a balm on Pigsy's bruises. He even thanked him for making the first sortie. He also suggested the need for a bit more tact and a more pleasing appearance. Pigsy transformed himself into a fat, dark, hairy, but jolly-looking monk and went back to the cavern. This time, he humbly referred to the female-monster soldiers as generals and pretended to be terrified of their weapons. So they spoke kindly to him:

"Don't worry, you're safe here. We aren't interested in tough, hairy, fat monks. Your meat would be too rancid for our refined tastes. Besides, our queen is preparing a wedding feast. She is about to marry a monk from the Tang Empire. Stay around and you may even get some leftovers."

Pigsy scampered off as the monster soldiers laughed at his surprisingly pig-like movements. Monkey thought about the news. As much as Monkey wanted to save Master, he preferred not to have to fight a thousand female-monster soldiers while doing so. So Monkey, Pigsy, and Sandy searched every inch of the mountain until they found a rock chimney that led from the interior of the cavern to the surface. Taking the form of a bat, Monkey flew down to the interior. It was so large that there was room for a large mansion and even a peach garden. Changing to the form of a green fly (there are always clouds of flies in monster caverns), he flew around until he found Master, locked inside an elegant room. There he changed back to his own shape. Master exclaimed:

"Buddha is merciful! You have found me. I should have listened to you. The young woman we rescued is the monster queen of this cavern. She told me that she is no ordinary monster, but the daughter of the Celestial Duke of the Southern Sky. She was bored in the Celestial Kingdom and came to earth to have some fun. She is an expert with a double sword and has told me if I don't marry her at the wedding feast tonight, I will be the main course for her feast."

Monkey asked Master to pretend to weaken to temptation and to share a cup of wine with her. Monkey would then transform himself into a dust mote floating in her cup. Once she drank him down, he would have her. So, Master called to the female guards to tell the queen that he agreed to be the husband. The queen monster was delighted, but she wasn't stupid. His sudden change of mind was very suspicious. When he proposed a toast, she examined her wine carefully. As soon as she spotted the dust-mote, she threw away the cup. Monkey then took the form of a giant eagle, seized Master by the shoulder and tried to fly out of the cavern. He was quick, but not quick enough. The queen's soldiers grabbed Master by the ankles. Short of tearing Master in half, Monkey couldn't get Master out. He let go, and fled.

Monkey, Pigsy, and Sandy worked out a better plan. They needed to make sure the monster queen would not become suspicious. Now, Monkey had noticed the peach garden. Peaches always gave Monkey ideas. He came to Master, again as a fly, with the new idea. To ease her suspicions, he suggested that Master flatter the queen and persuade her to walk with him in the peach garden. Monkey would transform himself into the pit in the best-looking peach on the tree. Master would pick it and take the first bite. He would offer the queen a bite. When she took her bite, Monkey would jump down her throat.

So Master called out again:

"Dear queen, you must admit that I have every reason to be scared and to escape. True, you are beautiful, but beauty alone is not enough for a marriage to work. The compatibility of spirits and souls is much more important. Tell me more about yourself. Give me some more time to get used to the idea of giving up my monk's status. After all, you know nothing of my habits. Let's get to know each other better."

Overjoyed, she let him out. First, she took him on a tour of the cavern. When they got to the peach garden, he asked if she would share a peach with him. He picked the best-looking peach, took a bite and handed it to her. As soon as she opened her mouth, Monkey leaped into her stomach.

Now he had her. He was very experienced with this trick, and knew just what to do. She could feel him poke about in her insides. She felt horrible pains shoot through her body. Just to make sure she understood, Monkey did a quick dance. She couldn't suffer any more of this. She agreed to release Master, and even carried him on her back to the outside of the cavern. When she had let Master go, Monkey, as promised, leaped out of her mouth.

"I'm really tired of all the extra trouble we've had because the Celestial Duke can't keep track of his daughter. In fact, the Celestial Kingdom doesn't seem able to keep their beasts, plants, and insects where they belong. Instead, we've had to cope with each of their failures. Why can't Celestial beings behave when they come down to earth instead of deciding to be monsters? It's time to make a formal complaint," grumbled Monkey.

Very steamed up, Monkey went straight to the Palace of the Celestial Duke of the Southern Regions. He rang the gong at the gate and loudly demanded an audience. The duke's soldiers would have attacked such an insolent monkey, but were stopped by their officers. The officers had not forgotten previous run-ins with the Great Saint Equal of Heaven. Monkey complained:

"You don't deserve to be duke. How can you rule a Celestial Realm? You can't even keep order in your own household. Your daughter has taken over as the Queen of the Bottomless Cavern and has already eaten one young monk. If I hadn't stopped her, she would certainly have eaten Master, or worse, forced him to marry her. What kind of a leader are you?"

This infuriated the Celestial Duke, who turned purple with anger:

"Rotten, filthy, ugly, beast! How dare you slander my children! Of course I know where my children are. My three sons and my only daughter have been at home with their mother. They haven't even left the palace gates. For this insult, I will personally petition the Celestial Emperor to have you flogged ten thousand times," he ranted. But before he could continue, one of his sons, whispered:

"Father, this Great Saint Equal of Heaven was able to hold all the emperor's troops at bay. Furthermore, he is on a holy mission for Kwan Yin. You'd better not get on his wrong side. Also, have you forgotten the daughter you adopted? Princess Camellia? Remember, you were taken by her charming voice and, instead of punishing her for forgetting to put oil in the altar lamps, you adopted her."

This deflated the Celestial Duke. Bowing politely to Monkey, he apologized for his harsh words. He admitted that he had forgotten about his adopted daughter, Princess Camellia, whom he had not seen for days. He offered to retrieve her. He and his sons came to her Cavern, calling for her.

She answered humbly, begging, "Please, don't punish me too harshly. I was just bored. I only ate one monk, and besides, it was his fault. He shouldn't have let himself be tempted away from the path of virtue."

This would never do. They bound her and took her to Heaven, where she was demoted and had to work as a scrubwoman.

CHAPTER 38

Danger to All Buddhist Monks

Danger awaits in a country that seeks to annihilate all Buddhist monks. The travelers are arrested despite their disguises. Monkey sets his hairs to act as barbers. All the men are shaven bald. The king repents. Monkey kills a were-fox.

The travelers continued on, with no serious incidents until they came to a country known as the "Country of No Laws." This didn't sound good. What did it mean? Was lawlessness prized? Were all the people lawless? They needed to know more. Pigsy was sent into the market place to pick up some gossip. As he loved to eat, have fun, and talk, he was a marvel at getting information out of people. Pretending to be a passing peddler, he learned that the country was once known as the "Country of True Law," but the king had a sudden change of heart, renamed it, and pronounced a death sentence on all of the country's ten thousand monks. Nine thousand, nine hundred and ninety-six had already been captured and were awaiting execution. He was delaying the execution until four monks from the Tang Empire arrived to make up the whole ten thousand. Then they would all be killed in one grand execution rite.

This was bad. There was no way to continue their journey without going through this country. Transforming himself into a bird, Monkey flew ahead to an inn. Here, four rich foreign merchants were asleep in its best room. Making himself invisible, he stole all their clothes and passports and returned to camp. Dressed in these clothes, the travelers hoped to avoid detection. Master, Monkey, Pigsy, and Sandy would go by the names Mr. Tang, Mr. Souen, Mr. Chu, and Mr. Sha. The baggage was transformed into a huge strongbox. In their disguises, they arrived at Traveler's Rest Inn at the capital. They registered in their new names and claimed to be horse merchants. However, they irritated the landlady when they ordered only a vegetarian meal. She didn't make much profit on meatless meals. She had never heard of rich merchants who were vegetarian. Maybe they really were Buddhist monks. Buddhist monks were vegetarian. There was a huge reward for anyone who turned in monks, especially the four monks expected from the Tang capital. She decided to tell the police about these vegetarian strangers.

The police raided the inn, arrested them, and seized the strongbox. Master, Monkey, Pigsy, and Sandy were put in chains and taken to prison. Master prepared for death, but Monkey told him not to worry. He transformed a thousand hairs into "sleep flies," which put everyone in the city to sleep. Then he transformed his hairs into barbers and had them shave the heads of all the men. Now, all the city's men looked like monks.

Pigsy ripped off the cell door, and they marched to the king's audience hall. The king had just awakened. He, too, had been shaven bald. His skull looked like an egg. Master asked the king, "What sins have these monks committed that you would order the execution of so many?"

The king was in shock over his shaved head and terrified at what he thought was the retribution of heaven. He admitted that a soothsayer had come to the palace a month ago and performed so many magical feats that the king believed he was truly an Immortal from Heaven. The soothsayer told the king that if he killed ten thousand monks, and drank a soup made from their hearts, he would achieve immortality. Eager for a short-cut to immortality, the king had all the kingdom's monks arrested.

He listened with remorse as Monkey told him, "True immortality does not come from magic or potions, but from living enough lives of virtue to ascend the scale of creation. You should have known that an evil deed cannot bring good." They called for the soothsayer, who tried to flee as soon as he saw Monkey. With one bound, Monkey leaped into the sky, hit him with his staff, and killed him. The soothsayer reverted to his true form, that of a white three-tailed fox. As soon he saw the body of the were-fox, the king woke from his enchantment.

All the monks in the kingdom were released, and the king changed the name of his country back to "Country of the True Law."

CHAPTER 39

Attack of Forty Monsters

Forty monsters try to ambush the pilgrims. Pigsy and Monkey put them to flight. The King of the Monsters tries to divide and conquer. Master is captured. A false head is given to the disciples to prove that Master is dead.

Their route seemed to go on forever. After passing through the Country of the True Law, they faced yet another mountain range. They could see lightning and a dark thundercloud ahead. So while Pigsy, Sandy, and Master made camp, Monkey leaped into the sky to check out the storm. Taking the form of an eagle, he flew right into the thundercloud. He expected to find a storm dragon doing its duty. But instead, there were forty monsters creating the storm. He could have killed them, but decided that killing forty lowly monster soldiers wouldn't do much for his reputation. Besides, it was Pigsy's turn to fight. But since Pigsy never volunteered to make any extra effort, he would have to trick him into doing his share.

Returning to camp, he sought out Pigsy:

"Well, brother Pig, it looks okay. There is a storm up ahead, although right now, it's only raining on a rich farmhouse where the people are preparing a huge feast. Looked like lots of stir-fried goodies. Almond cakes were all over the place. Some of that dark cloud is actually just smoke from their ovens."

That got Pigsy's attention. He was always hungry. He often grumbled that, unlike Master, Monkey, and Sandy, who seemed perfectly content with three grains of rice a day, he needed to eat like the big, strong pig that he was. Right now, his stomach felt like a hollow gourd. He wouldn't mind getting to that farmhouse and having first dibs on the goodies. So he volunteered to go on ahead, mentioning a need to cut forage for their horse. In order not to petrify any passers-by with fear, took the form of a jolly, dark and fat monk.

But it wasn't a farm house, but the nest of the forty monsters, all of whom thought pork would be a nice addition to their dinner. Pigsy realized that he had been tricked by Monkey, but there was nothing he could do except fight. Fighting forty monsters was hard work. Pigsy began to have the worst of it. But Monkey had been watching from the clouds above and leaped down to help. The two of them quickly defeated the monsters.

Pigsy was furious at Monkey's trick, but he did enjoy a good fight now and then. After all, Monkey hadn't deserted him. So he acknowledged his little maneuver, and forgave Monkey. Once again the best of brothers, they returned to camp to brag about how they had driven off the monsters.

The forty monsters who fled the nest returned to their main cavern. They told their leader that they would have been able to capture the Monk from the Tang Empire except for a ferocious Pig Being and a ferocious Monkey Being who almost killed all of them. One of the monster generals was a refugee from another monster cavern that Monkey had destroyed in an encounter many months ago. He warned that the Monkey disciple was too powerful to beat in a face-to-face duel. Another general, who had studied the art of war in the Tang Empire, suggested that the only way to capture Master was to divide the disciples. If three of their strongest generals ambushed the cavalcade, each attacking one of Master's disciples, King of the Monsters would have a chance to capture Master.

Meanwhile, the travelers were moving on. When they reached a mountain pass, the three monster generals and their troops ambushed them. Each general had a target, as planned. While Monkey, Pigsy, and Sandy fought in the skies above, the King of the Monsters sneaked into the camp, threw a blanket over Master, and carried him back to the cavern. Master was (once again) put into a cage. The monster king decided to wait a few days before eating him. After the disciples were defeated and would not be returning to save Master, the monsters could eat him in peace.

It didn't take Monkey long to recognize the "divide and conquer" tactic being used against them. He made quick work of the troops attacking him, joined Pigsy, and put Pigsy's opponents to flight. Then the two of them joined Sandy and beat back all Sandy's attackers. They also captured a monster general who revealed that Master had been taken to the Cavern of Stalactites in the Mountain of Fogs.

Leaping into the clouds, they were able to spot the noxious vapor emanating from the Cavern of Stalactites. There, Monkey, Pigsy, and Sandy gave the monsters a choice.

"Release Master or fight!"

The monsters, on the advice of one of the monster king's advisors, carved a head from willow wood. It looked just like Master. Presenting it to Monkey, they said:

"What has been done, cannot be undone. Unable to resist the tempting aroma of your Master, we ate him raw. Only his head remains. We humbly beg your forgiveness, and offer you his head for honorable burial."

Master had truly loved his disciples. They also loved him. Monkey, Pigsy, and Sandy wept. They took the head and burned it on a funeral pyre. Now that they didn't have Master to tell them to forgive their enemies, they decided on revenge. Monkey used his power of "Multiplication of Hordes" to convert his hairs into thousands of soldiers. The monsters saw them coming and barricaded the cavern mouth with an enormous boulder.

When a frontal attack fails, it's time to look for weak areas on the flanks. Carefully scouting the area, inch by inch, Sandy found a small hole leading to the inside of the cave. Taking the form of a rat, Monkey entered, while Pigsy and Sandy distracted the monsters with yells, screams, and rock-bashing. Monkey was delighted when he found that Master was alive and well. He changed to a fly, flew to Master's ear, and whispered to him not to be afraid. Then scurrying around as a rat, he went to spy on the monsters. They were having a heated discussion of recipes. Some were for steaming, some for frying, and a few argued that roasted monk tasted the best. Monkey released his "sleep flies" and put them all to sleep. Then, transforming himself into a giant monkey, he used his staff as a lever and rolled the huge rock from the cavern mouth. Master was saved. All recipe questions were resolved when Monkey set the cavern on fire, roasting all the monsters.

Chapter 40

Virtue Ends a Drought

In the Country of the Phoenix, a crime against Heaven results in drought. Monkey urges the prince to take the path of virtue and obtains rain.

After crossing the Mountains of the South, they came to a fortified city in the Country of the Phoenix. The region had suffered from a terrible drought for the past three years. The countryside was bare of crops and animals. The few people they saw looked like skeletons and begged food from them. The streets of the city were deserted. At the local inn, where even gold could not buy food or drink, they saw a proclamation from the king that declared a rain-making contest. The winner would be given any treasure he or she wanted, even the whole kingdom.

When Master presented his credentials to the king, he also offered to have Monkey enter the contest, not for a reward, but just to help. On the eve of the contest, Monkey went up into the clouds to talk to the local rain dragon:

"Look Brother Dragon, I can see why there must be an occasional drought, just to give you some rest if nothing else. But why three years? Tomorrow, when I try to make it rain, I'll need your help to end the drought."

The dragon replied:

"Normally, I would be happy to rain torrents for you, Great Saint Equal of Heaven, but my orders for the drought came straight from the Celestial Emperor and I have no authority to change them. You know what he does to disobedient subjects. After all, that's one of the reasons the Tang Emperor sent you on this journey. If you convince the Celestial Emperor to change his mind, I'll be happy to obey."

So Monkey had to fly all the way to the Celestial Palace and ask permission to speak to the Celestial Emperor. As usual, he was quickly admitted. No one there had ever forgotten Monkey's successes as a rebel Great Saint Equal of Heaven. The emperor explained that three years ago, the King of the Country of Phoenix had committed sacrilege. He had allowed his dogs to eat offerings intended for Heaven that had been placed on an altar. The punishment would end when rats ate a mountain of rice in the Celestial Emperor's courtyard, when a dog ate the mountain of flour in the granary, and when the gold chain strung across the gate shattered. Then if the king took up the Path of Virtue, Heaven would show mercy.

Monkey wasn't sure he understood all this. He returned and told Master the whole story. The king admitted that three years ago, indeed the dogs had eaten the offerings, but it was not intentional. In an argument with the queen, the king had overturned a tripod, which then overturned the altar, spilling the offerings onto the floor, where his guard dogs ate them. He offered his life to the Celestial Emperor if his people could be spared the drought. If allowed to live, he promised to make amends and to adopt the path of virtue thereafter. His repentance was enough to immediately spur the rats to eat the rice, the dog to eat the flour, and to shatter the gold chain. Not only did the rains begin, but the storehouses in the Kingdom became magically filled overnight with rice and flour, and the treasury with gold.

Chapter 41

Attacked by Lions

The disciples arrive in the Country of Jade. Their weapons are used as models for human weapons but are stolen. The Nine-Headed Lion, Yellow Lion, and five other lion monsters attack. Master, the king, and Pigsy are captured. Blue Star lassoes the lions.

As another autumn came to a close, the travelers arrived in the Province of Jade, in the Country of Bamboo. This country was known for its prosperity and the virtue of its prince. It was much like the Tang Empire, with magnificent buildings, great temples, and cultured citizens. Master was greeted with honor when he presented his credentials. At a state banquet, he was pressed again and again to tell of his fourteen years of travel to the West and praised for his devotion. Monkey, Pigsy, and Sandy were given seats in places of honor and treated very well, though as usual, many people were put off by their odd appearance. Now, while Master had fine manners suitable even in the highest levels of the Tang Empire, his disciples were far from polished. As the wine began to flow, Monkey became a bit loud, Pigsy began to belch, and Sandy started to snore.

When the three sons of the king saw this, they lost their temper. Arming themselves, they attacked Monkey, Pigsy, and Sandy. Immediately, the three pulled out their weapons. Of course, these magical weapons shone with an unearthly light. The sons were stunned, and they knelt in apology before such superior supernatural beings. To their credit, the three disciples did recognize that they had been rude. In apology they agreed to teach the princes the use of weapons similar to their own.

(Their own, of course, were too heavy to even be lifted by humans.)

So, while Master rested as an honored guest of the king, Monkey, Pigsy, and Sandy taught the princes weapon skills. They brought their own precious weapons (iron staff, rake, and trident) to a tower where the king's blacksmiths would make prince-size copies. Away from their owners, the weapons shined even more brightly, emitting a brilliant light visible for hundreds of li.

When Yellow Lion, the monster who lived in the Tiger Jaw Cavern on Leopard Mountain, spotted the glow, he saw his opportunity. He sent a furious dust storm to the capital. As the dust storm raged, sending everyone indoors, he flew to the tower and stole the weapons.

Eventually the dust storm subsided and Monkey noticed the weapons were gone. He knew the blacksmiths weren't responsible. A human could not even lift these weapons. Only a monster could be the thief. Could it be the one living in the Tiger Mouth Cavern, the princes wondered? Monkey, weaponless, flew to the cavern in the form of a bird and perched on a tree to spy. Two servant monsters came to eat their noonday meal under the shade of the tree. The first said:

"Our Master is certainly fortunate. In addition to his recent capture of a beautiful girl, he stole three precious weapons. There'll be feasting tonight. In fact, good friend, I cheated when I was buying the master's provisions. We'll have a little extra silver to use for a party of our own afterwards."

"Wonderful! I can bring some great food and wine to our party as I short-changed the chef when I was 'helping' him. But it will still be a lot of work tonight at the Feast of the Rake," replied the second.

Monkey immediately said his "fix in place" spell, moved them far away, took their clothes, the silver, and their identity medallions which said "Wily Demon" and "Clever-Fingered Demon." Returning to the capital for Pigsy and Sandy, he gave the silver to the blacksmiths to pay for their work. He and Pigsy took the forms of Wily Demon and Clever-Fingered Demon. Sandy took the form of a cattle herder, as the monsters were expecting cattle deliveries for their Feast of the Rake. Once at the cave, they joined in the setting-up duties. All went well, until Pigsy saw his rake carried out to be the centerpiece of the banquet. With a great shout, he seized his weapon. Monkey and Sandy called to their own weapons. The iron staff and trident flew into their hands and the fight began. The monster and his generals were no match for Monkey, Pigsy, and Sandy. As they fled, Monkey torched the cavern.

Master, the king, and the three princes were overjoyed at their success. The king was worried, though. Would the monsters attack once Master, Monkey, Pigsy, and Sandy left?

Meanwhile, Yellow Lion fled to his grandfather, the Nine-headed Lion, for help. His grandfather knew about the monk from the Tang Empire and his three powerful disciples. He needed reinforcement, so he called in his other five grandsons, Lion Monkey, Snow Lion, Tiger Lion, Gold Lion, and Red Lion. The grandsons all converged on grandfather's home, the Cavern of Nine Chambers on the Mountain of Bamboo Knots. Brandishing their weapons, they rushed to Yellow Lion's cavern, but it was too late. They found nothing but dead monsters and ashes. Under cover of an enormous storm, they came to the capital city to seek revenge.

At the gates of the palace, the lion monsters threatened to kill all the people in the city unless Monkey, Pigsy, and Sandy came out to fight. Of course the three disciples took the challenge and fought. The battle was terrible. They fought all day and all night, but neither side won.

Now, the monsters had their own special weapons. Yellow Lion had a three-bladed sword, Lion Monkey had a mace, and Snow Lion had a hammer. Tiger Lion had a lance, Gold Lion an ax, and Red Lion a cudgel. The Nine-Headed Lion was armed with eighteen swords, spears, and cords, for each of his hands.

In the battle, Monkey and Sandy captured Tiger Lion and Snow Lion. But on the second day of combat, Snow Lion escaped and hit Pigsy on the back with his hammer, knocked the wind out of him and captured him. And the Nine-Headed Lion entered the palace and captured Master, the king, and his sons, while five of the six lion grandsons were fighting the three disciples.

Monkey used one of his diversion tricks, transforming one hair into a false Monkey and another into false Sandy. He and Sandy flew away on a cloud while the fake ones flew away in another direction.

At dawn Monkey and Sandy returned to the Cavern of Bamboo Knots to challenge the Nine-Headed Lion and his remaining grandsons to more combat. The Nine-Headed Lion led the attack, repelling each of Monkey and Sandy's attacks. He finally cornered them inside the cavern, but Monkey expelled a tremendous breath, blowing out all the lanterns.

In the dark, he and Sandy escaped. But Master and Pigsy were still captive. Tiger-Lion snuck away in the confusion.

"The closer we get to India, the more powerful the monsters get," thought Monkey. He needed help, and powerful help, at that. He and Sandy sent a messenger to Chang Ti, the Celestial Emperor, to ask for his assistance. Chang Ti ordered a quick count of all the heavenly beings. It was discovered that at the palace of the Blue Star Constellation, a stable hand had gotten drunk, forgotten to chain the lions, and they had escaped. Blue Star came down immediately to the Cavern of Bamboo Knots and joined Monkey and Sandy. From the mouth of the cavern, Monkey shouted a challenge to combat. The Nine-Headed Lion and all six grandsons charged out, thinking Monkey was alone and that he would be easy to kill. Monkey pretended to weaken and to flee into the clouds. As soon as the monster lions drew close to his hiding place, Blue Star threw out seven lassos, snagging the lions. The lassos immediately changed to harnesses, and the lions back to their lion-forms. Remembering their duties as mounts, they crawled to Blue Star's feet and begged his forgiveness. Monkey and Sandy charged into the cavern, freed the king, his sons, Master, Pigsy, and all the other prisoners. Now the kingdom was safe, and the pilgrims could continue onwards with an easy conscience.

CHAPTER 42

Tested by Fake Buddhas

At the Feast of Lanterns in the City of Golden Peace, Master mistakenly pays homage to monsters disguised as Buddhas. They capture Master, Pigsy, and Sandy. Monkey asks for Celestial help. The Four Star Beings capture the monsters.

After ten days of travel, they came to a large city, the City of Golden Peace. It seemed to be a holiday. The streets were packed with crowds.

Whenever the travelers arrived in a city, they would find their way to the nearest temple. Master would first visit the main temple, begging for permission to pray in the temple's main hall. As usual, he would explain to the monks that his ferocious and odd-looking companions were in fact holy brothers in religion. Master would ask for permission to fulfill his vow of sweeping all the temple towers.

Today, the abbot in charge of the Monastery of Sublime Goodness invited them to stay for the Feast of Lanterns. It celebrated, he said, an annual event in which three Buddhas would descend from heaven to the temple and drink holy oil from the temple lanterns for three nights. Hearing this, Master begged for permission to spend the night in front of the lanterns to await their arrival. Indeed, that very evening, a high wind arose, though the lanterns continued to burn brightly. Then three Buddhas descended onto the temple in a bright halo to take the oil. Master, kneeling before them, began a prayer of thanksgiving. Just then, in bounded Monkey.

"Master! Get up! I've met a fair number of Buddhas and none of them drink lantern oil. I've been suspicious all along. These are demons in disguise."

As Master tried to collect his wits, the false "Buddhas" finished drinking the oil and blew out a cloud of dense, black, oily smoke. Monkey was temporarily blinded, and he frantically rubbed his eyes. The "Buddhas" grabbed Master and disappeared. While Pigsy and Sandy watched over their goods, Monkey went out to search, leaping into the sky. He searched for hours, finding nothing unusual until he noticed that all the trees around Blue Dragon Mountain were dead. He swooped in for a closer look, spotting a cavern with the name "Black Flower Cavern" carved over the entrance. Transforming himself into a cat, Monkey sneaked into the cavern.

An old monster-servant was lecturing new monster-servants on their duties:

"You are fortunate indeed to find employment with our three kings, the Prince of Cold, the Prince of Heat, and the Prince of Dust. There isn't much work and the princes have lived for centuries thanks to the holy oil offered by the inhabitants of this country. Tonight, all you have to do is to wash the monk from the Tang Empire carefully, make him eat some spices and sage, and then marinate him an hour in a mixture of soy paste and wine. The chef will do the cooking."

Monkey quickly sneaked back out of the cavern to get Pigsy and Sandy.

Pounding on the cavern gates with his staff, he thundered:

"False Buddhas, release this Holy Monk, who comes from the Tang Empire. He has been traveling for fourteen years to bring back Holy Scriptures for the Tang Emperor"

The three princes charged out with their monster soldiers, a gang of large transcendent rhinos. One prince was armed with a mace, one with a lance, and the third with a skewer. These monster princes and their soldiers had hides so thick that Monkey's staff had no effect. Pigsy's rake didn't scratch them and Sandy's trident couldn't stab through them. After a day of combat, they had to retire.

That evening Monkey transformed himself into a firefly and flew into the cavern with a swarm of local fireflies. He found Master and untied him, but before he could carry him out, some monster soldiers saw him and he had to leave Master behind. The three monster princes now barricaded themselves in the cavern. They sent out a monster raiding party that captured Pigsy and Sandy.

Once again, Monkey had to turn to the Celestial Realm for help. He asked the Pole Star Saint, who explained:

"These are indeed very powerful demons. Only the Four Star Beings (the Crocodile Star, the Lobster Star, the Wolf Star, and the Hyena Star) who live in the Big Dipper Constellation can prevail against these monsters. They are the only ones with weapons that can pierce any hide, even transcendent rhino hides."

Monkey lost no time in begging the Star Beings to help. Now accompanied by the Pole Star Saint and the four Star Beings, he returned to the cavern just as the monsters had almost finished marinating Master, Pigsy, and Sandy. When the three princes saw the stellar generals, they knew they were outmatched and fled to the nearest river, but were countered by the river dragons, who joined the Heavenly troops. The Prince of Cold, the Prince of Heat, and the Prince of Dust then tried to run in different directions, but were captured with celestial lassos provided by the Hyena Star and thrown by the Crocodile Star, the Lobster Star, and the Wolf Star. Monkey asked the Star Beings to bring the captured monsters to the temple so the people could see how they had been fooled. Then the prisoners were led away for Celestial judgment.

The people in the kingdom were delighted at being shown the truth. They replaced the Feast of Lanterns with the Feast of the Holy Monks. They even had a parade with dancers wearing Master, Monkey, Pigsy, and Sandy masks. Pigsy would have been happy to stay for a year of feasts, but Master ordered them to resume their voyage again in three days.

Chapter 43

Tested by a False Princess

A temple harbors a woman claiming to be the real princess of the kingdom. Master is chosen by the false princess to be her husband. He pretends to agree. The disciples pretend to leave. Monkey returns and unmasks a hare that escaped from the Celestial Realm.

In the Southern Wilderness, they came to a large and very rich temple, with the words "Temple of Gold Flowers" carved over the gate. This was near the border of the Nation of Wei, famous for its riches. It was rumored that the capital city's streets were paved with gold. The local abbot greeted the voyagers kindly and arranged an enormous vegetarian feast for them. The monks were clever cooks. They served "beef," "duck," "shrimp," and "chicken" dishes, all made from soybeans, and looking and tasting almost like the real thing. Pigsy had never felt so satisfied. Master had never seen a temple so rich. Every Buddha was encrusted with jewels. The abbot explained that all this wealth had been given to them by the king, who was very devout.

In the temple garden, they heard a young woman weeping. The abbot hastened to explain:

"This is not a corrupt temple that keeps women. A year ago, one of our monks found this young woman by the roadside. It was months before she was restored to health, and her mind seems to be gone. She insists that she is really the princess of this country who was kidnapped by a monster while walking in the garden. We sent messengers to the capital to ask if the princess was missing and were told that she was right there, and as beautiful as ever. Clearly our visitor is out of her mind. But we cannot abandon her. So we keep her here, locked in this isolated tower."

When Master and Monkey met her, they didn't think she was mad, even though she wept rivers. They determined to find out more when they came to the capital.

When they went to the court to present their credentials, even they were surprised by the wealth of the citizens. There was a festive air. Large numbers of young men were on horseback riding around a tower. Apparently, the princess was to choose her husband that very day by throwing a silken ball down from the tower. Whoever it hit would become her husband. The crowds were so heavy that Monkey and Master were temporarily separated. Just as Monkey was making his way toward Master, a silk ball sailed over all the young mens' heads and landed right on Master's shoulder. Not only that, it stuck there and he couldn't remove it. Monkey couldn't get to him without trampling innocent by-standers, so Master made a hand signal to him to return to the temple and to wait for further orders.

Master was brought to the palace. Despite all his protests, he was told to prepare for a wedding. He would either be married to the princess or his head and body would be separated. Master was clever as well as good-hearted. After all, he'd been in this situation before, and, with the help of his disciples, managed to escape in one piece. He politely explained that he had no problems with doing his duty by the princess but he needed to have his disciples brought before him so that he could give them specific orders on how to finish his mission.

The king's chamberlain was sent to the Temple of Gold Flowers to invite Monkey, Pigsy, and Sandy to court. Once they were alone with Master, he explained what had happened and how, on the 12th of that month, he would be forced to marry the "princess." Monkey could not tell if this was even the real princess. So far, she had kept her face hidden behind a thick veil. She might be a monster, but she had not yet shown any supernatural powers.

At the engagement feast, Master pretended to be delighted. Pigsy ate all he could. Sandy sat quietly and Monkey kept alert. He noticed that the princess seemed to be actively avoiding him. Her aura kept changing colors, sometimes bright, sometimes dark. She kept complaining that she didn't want Master's fierce-looking disciples near her. The king's complexion was ashen, a sure sign he was under the influence of a were-beast. Right before the wedding, the king issued passports for Pigsy, Sandy, and Monkey. They pretended to leave, with much hand waving, bowing, and tears, to continue Master's journey, according to his instructions. But Monkey transformed one of his hairs into his double, and flew back to the palace in the shape of an eagle. Now in the shape of a cricket, he hopped into Master's room, and informed Master that the princess was indeed a were-being of some sort or a monster. While they were talking, the princess opened the door. Monkey, resuming his own form, challenged her to single combat. She flew into the sky, using a large pestle as her weapon. Monkey followed her, and they fought fiercely. Finally, he had her cornered right in front of the Temple of Gold Flowers. Just as he was about to pulverize her with his staff, he heard a voice from the sky.

"Stop!" pleaded the Stellar Princess of the Yin (Princess of the Female Principle). "That's my pet hare. I let it escape in a moment of absent-mindedness."

She hadn't done anything very evil. Monkey was willing to let her live, provided she made a full confession to the court and restored the true princess to her rightful place. This was quickly done. Master was, once again, saved from marriage, and they could now continue with their journey.

Chapter 44

A False Accusation

Master and his disciples are wrongly accused of the murder of a benefactor. Monkey convinces the widow to recant her false accusation. They are all released. Monkey retrieves the soul of their benefactor from the Underworld. All ends well.

It was autumn again. Everyone was tired from sleeping in the open and was delighted to reach a town. Just inside the city gates, they found a large palace with an inscription carved over the door, "Lodging for Ten Thousand Monks". The gatekeeper explained that Lord Yuan owned the palace. The Lord was a white-haired old man of sixty-four. When he was a lad, some monks had saved his life. In gratitude, he vowed that he would provide lodging for the next ten thousand monks that he encountered. He had already given shelter to 9,996 monks. Now, with the arrival of the four travelers, his vow would be fulfilled.

After the Feast of the Fulfilled Vows, Master, Monkey, Pigsy, and Sandy continued on, despite repeated invitations from their host and hostess to stay at least a week. The four monks were very close now to their destination, Ling Shan, where they would find the True Scriptures. The whole countryside had heard that they were coming and all were ready to welcome them.

They had no sooner left than a robber band raided the palace of Lord Yuan, killed him, and stole all his treasures. Lady Yuan was heartbroken. She blamed Master and his disciples for his death. She believed that if they had stayed on the robbers would not have succeeded, and she swore vengeance on them. Lord and Lady Yuan had had two sons late in life. These young men were brilliant scholars and loving sons. Lady Yuan was so angry that she lied, telling her sons that Master and his disciples had been scouts for the brigands. The sons then made a formal complaint to the king.

Completely unaware of all this, Master and his disciples continued on their way. They soon entered territory controlled by the robber band. The brigands were sure they must have gold and silver, and leaped out of the woods to attack them. Monkey used his fix-in-place spell to immobilize them. He then questioned them and discovered that they had robbed and murdered Lord Yuan. So, Master, Monkey, Pigsy, and Sandy turned back to return the stolen treasure to Lord Yuan's family. Just as they arrived at Lord Yuan's home, they were arrested by the king's soldiers. A crooked judge refused to hear any defense, though he made it clear they could go if they gave him all their loot.

Fearing that they would torture Master to get a confession, Monkey declared,

"I am the guilty one here. Torture me!"

It was no use. The crooked judge threw them all in jail anyway.

Monkey escaped in the form of a mouse, converting one of his hairs into a place-holding image of himself. He ran back to Lord Yuan's residence, where the Lord's funeral was being prepared. He quickly changed himself into a termite, and chewed his way into the coffin. From the inside he called out to the lord's wife and sons, using Lord Yuan's voice:

"Why did you do this to the four innocent travelers? Your lies will keep me chained on earth, languishing as an unhappy ghost. Tell the truth."

Hearing this, Lady Yuan came to her senses.

"I must have been temporarily insane," she thought. "Instead of putting the blame on the evildoers, I lied and blamed the monks. I believed they could have prevented all this."

She told her sons the truth. They ran to the palace to save Master and his disciples.

In the meantime, Monkey, in the form of a bird, went to the Grand Inquisitor's residence. Using the voice of the Inquisitor's long-dead father, he ordered the four innocent monks to be freed. The dazed Grand Inquisitor rushed to the jail. Monkey, also returning to the jail, now told

Master, "Don't bow when the guards come to get you. Don't act like a prisoner, act like a lord."

Lady Yuan and her sons had been trying to tell the corrupt judge the truth. He refused to listen and was about to throw them out. When the Grand Inquisitor arrived and heard Lady Yuan's story, he ordered the corrupt judge jailed. He personally released Master, Monkey, Pigsy, and Sandy. Soldiers who were sent to the forest found the brigands, still frozen like statues, and brought them back for trial.

Monkey felt badly that their benefactor had been killed, so he returned to the Shadowlands and asked to check the records. There he saw that the death date for Lord Yuan was set at the 12th day of the 12th year of the reign. When the clerk wasn't looking, Monkey took a writing brush and changed the 12th year to the 22nd year. So Lord Yuan's soul was returned. Even better, he would have another ten years of life. As no one had died, the robbers were only sentenced to ten years of hard labor, which would give them a chance to reform.

CHAPTER 45

The Journey Ends

They arrive at Buddha's Temple of Thunder in India. Their bodies are left behind. Their souls continue. They bring the True Scriptures back to the Tang Empire and to all the temples on the way. Monkey becomes a "pou sa," a lesser Buddha. Pigsy gets his old position back and so does Sandy. The Horse resumes life as a dragon. The beheaded dragon is reborn as a prince. The quest ends with success.

At last they were in India. As they neared Ling Shan, the mountain where Buddha's Temple of Thunder was located, the country grew more and more beautiful. In a month, they covered the eight hundred li to the foot of Ling Shan. Here they met the Immortal Kin Ting. He urged them never to lose heart no matter what strange barriers they encountered. Following the bright halo that wreathed the mountain, they came to an immense river at the base of the mountain. A ferry was moored to a pier.

A sign said, "All who would cross this river must go by this ferry."

The boat had no bottom, yet floated in the water. The boatman was shrouded in a halo of light. Taking courage from Kin Ting's advice, Master stepped into the boat. Just as his foot touched the water, he felt himself stumble. Pigsy and Sandy also stumbled. Only Monkey did not stumble. Suddenly, Master saw some bodies floating in the water. Looking closely, he realized that the bodies looked just like Pigsy, Sandy, and him. What were they to make of this?

Monkey explained: "Don't be disturbed. I recognized the boatman. This is the river that separates the Celestial from the Earthly realms. No

being of flesh-and-blood can cross this river. Only the soul can cross because it is eternal. You, Pigsy, and Sandy merely left behind your fleshly envelopes. I, however, was born of a stone and so was not affected."

Master saw that his disciples were each surrounded by a brilliant aura, as was he. The Horse had returned to its true form as a dragon. Monkey's gold circle had vanished as Kwan Yin had promised. Now they flew directly to the peak of the mountain. They entered the Temple of Thunder, where all the Immortals were assembled to greet them. Buddha presided over the welcome. Thousands of heavenly beings—from saints to sweepers—cheered the Pilgrims. Buddha personally presented them with copies of the True Scriptures, which had been created especially for those in the Middle Kingdom to read. (The heavenly versions were of pure light and could only be understood by heavenly beings).

Their pilgrimage had taken fifteen years. Their return to the Tang Empire could have taken fifteen seconds, but they decided to stop at each of the places where they had defeated monsters or where humans had helped. To avoid scaring everyone with their brilliant celestial halos and to make sure they were recognized, they resumed their former shapes. They were careful to stop at each temple along their route and to leave behind a copy of the True Text. They even found the large turtle that had helped them cross a river and gave him a copy. They also had the answer he was seeking. Indeed, in his next reincarnation, he would be rewarded for his virtuous deeds and he would ascend to a higher level of being.

As they grew near the Tang Empire's borders, they were quickly spotted. The Tang Emperor had had watchtowers built just to look for their return. Soldiers used mirrors and signal fires to relay the good news to Chang An, the capital. When they entered the capital, even the Tang Emperor knelt to them. Master handed over the True Scriptures, but he warned the Empire's monks that all the study of scriptures in the world was worth nothing if monks did not truly lead pure lives. Only then would their prayers help those awaiting rebirth in the Shadowlands. Monkey King, Pigsy, and Sandy were equally honored as true disciples. Pigsy especially enjoyed the many banquets. Sandy even smiled on occasion and stopped quoting the one thousand rules of correct behavior. Monkey could hardly contain either his happiness or his impatience to return to the Celestial Realms.

Finally, Monkey was able to persuade Master, Pigsy, and Sandy that it was time to leave. They asked the Tang Emperor to call the entire court to the temple. Master gave a short sermon urging all of them to lead pure lives, to treat others as they would want to be treated, and to pay as much attention to the health of their souls as they did to the health of their bodies. The Emperor and his ministers made speeches of thanks. Finally, the Pilgrims allowed their auras to become visible. Soon, the halos grew so bright that everyone in the temple covered their eyes. When they opened them again, the Pilgrims had gone. (Decades later, people in the capital and the countryside would still talk of the day of great light.)

Now back in the Celestial Kingdom, the Pilgrims bowed before Buddha. Buddha tapped Master on the head. Suddenly Master remembered his past life. Then, he had been a disciple of Buddha who had volunteered to undertake this task because of the compassion he felt for human suffering. With the journey complete, Master returned to his true role in the Celestial Realm. He would be Kwan Yin's Chief Disciple, with special responsibility for compassionate acts to ease suffering. As he had hoped long ago, Monkey King was made a pou sa (Lesser Buddha). He still preferred to be known as the Great Saint Equal of Heaven Monkey King. He would always be particularly sympathetic to boys and girls who couldn't sit still and were occasionally naughty. He would also retain his power over all horses.

Pigsy was given his old position back. Although he still loved food and drink, he was careful to avoid annoying the Celestial Handmaidens. And he retained a special sympathy for those who enjoyed the good things in life.

Sandy, who had been the sobersides of the journey, was happy to be restored to his original post as Official of Screens. He set to work at once, making sure all regulations on screen size, shape, and color were properly obeyed. The dragon that had helped them as the Horse was given a position as the Dragon Marshall of the Second Palace. And the dragon whose decapitation and whose plea to the Emperor started this whole saga was rewarded. His soul was released from the Shadowlands and he was reborn as a handsome young prince who found the path to virtue.

So ends the journey but not the saga. There will always be evils and monsters to fight. There will also be good people to save. Monkey, Pigsy, and Sandy may occasionally decide that it would be fun to descend to earth as their former selves and as brothers-in-arms. Use your imagination and you can add the stories of those adventures.